I0623864

Donahue

FOSTER'S PRIDE BOOK 2

KATHI S. BARTON

This is a work of fiction. Names, characters, places, and incidents are products of the author's imagination or are used fictitiously and are not to be construed as real. Any resemblance to actual events, locations, organizations, or persons, living or dead, is entirely coincidental.

World Castle Publishing, LLC
Pensacola, Florida
Copyright © Kathi S. Barton 2020
Paperback ISBN: 9781951642914
eBook ISBN: 9781951642921
First Edition World Castle Publishing, LLC, July 6, 2020
http://www.worldcastlepublishing.com
Licensing Notes
All rights reserved. No part of this book may be used or reproduced in any manner whatsoever without written permission, except in the case of brief quotations embodied in articles and reviews.
Cover: Karen Fuller
Editor: Maxine Bringenberg

Chapter 1

Parker didn't move when the warden came to stand in front of her cell. She'd learned a few things while being incarcerated. One of them—and it hadn't taken her long to figure this one out—was that she was never in the right. Also, in this case, she wasn't to talk or move toward the cell door until they said she could.

"Miss Carter?" She turned and looked at the speaker from her position on the floor. Carter had been doing push-ups when she heard the footsteps coming toward her cell. "I'm to tell you that you're going to be set free today. They proved you didn't kill your father."

She was sure it was a joke. For the last eight years, she'd been saying she'd not killed him. It had been tempting, on a daily basis, to get rid of him. However, she'd not been the one who murdered him.

Standing up, she saw Warden Peck back away, as if she could reach him through the bars she'd come to call her front door. She could, actually, not just reach him, but leave the jail without anyone knowing. However, Parker didn't. Without a word from her, she was handed a bag as well as a checklist. Inside the bag was the bloodied clothing she'd come here in, as well as her possessions. Not much of it would do her any good now, but she stripped down right there and pulled the jeans and shirt on while the men turned their backs to her.

"You could at least have waited until we were gone to do that." Standing back when they asked her if she was finished, she waited as they unlocked the cell door. "There is some paperwork we have to have you sign. Also, because you were wrongly accused, there will be some money coming to you. Do you have any questions so far?"

"No."

She followed the three men, two of them guards she'd had extraordinarily little to do with since arriving here eight years ago, and was taken into a smallish room where her attorney was waiting, as well as two people she'd never thought to see again—her aunt and uncle on her father's side of the family.

"They have it in their heads that you didn't kill my brother. I still don't believe it, but then they never asked me for permission to let you out of here, where you belong. But I told them that you'd be back. Soon too, if I know you well enough." Parker said neither of them knew her. "I know you well enough to know that even though they said you didn't kill him, you were a part of his death. I'll always believe that of you."

As they said their piece, however incorrect they were, Parker kept her mouth shut. She wasn't what they thought she was—a person with very few morals and no sense of the laws of the land. Instead, she was an immensely powerful being—mostly, she reasoned, because of her mom.

Few people, including the few she'd shared a cell with over her time here, had any idea what she and her parents were. As she waited for the paperwork, Parker thought of the things she was going to have to do when she was out. First and foremost, she had to figure out how she'd ended up in here.

Given a few minutes alone with her only living relatives, Parker wondered why they had been called. Or, for that matter, why they'd even bothered with her at all. It wasn't until she was given the first thing to sign that she knew. They were supposed to be helping her acclimate herself to the outside world.

Signing her name to the places marked, she didn't bother asking questions. She might get some of them answered, but not to her satisfaction, that she could count on. Standing up, she was asked to sign the list stating that she'd received all her belongings from when she was arrested. Parker had a feeling she was going to have to figure out her own way home. Aunt Mae and Uncle Raymond left her standing by the open gates to her freedom.

"You can press charges if you want. They're supposed to keep you in their home for a few weeks." Parker told the guard, Mary, she didn't want to be around them. "Yes, I guess I can understand that. They were at your hearing, the one where it was figured out you couldn't have killed your dad. I never heard such language from anyone in my life as I did when your aunt started screaming at the lawyers how you had to be guilty. She's a piece of cake, isn't she?"

She and Mary had gone to school at the same time. It was funny to her that Mary had gone into law enforcement and been on the opposite side of the cells. Mary and her brother Thomas had gotten into more trouble before breakfast than a hardened criminal would in all his life.

After Thomas had been killed, gunned down by a man who thought he had been having an affair with his wife, Mary had taken a good look at her life and changed. Not once in the ten years he'd been gone, had Mary ever slipped back into her dangerous role. Parker had been with her when the news came that Thomas was gone. It had hurt the two of them more than it had when her father's life was taken.

"Do you know what you're going to do now, Parker?" Shrugging was answer enough for her friend. "I'm going to miss having you around. Honestly, it's what made me want to come to work every day. And I've been making some money off the investments you've been having me do for you. Do you have a way to get to the halfway house, or do you need a ride?"

"I'll walk." Mary told her it was a good ten miles. "I'll walk. It's not that far."

It wouldn't feel like it either. Parker had been into fitness as well as self-defense since before they'd arrested her and had been able to keep up with it after being put in prison. There was a nice treadmill she thought no one but her used in the fitness room. Weights too. Even in the time allotted to her for being out of doors, Parker had walked the fence line every day she could. It was the only reprieve she'd ever had from being locked up.

Mary had been taking care of little things for her since she'd been assigned to a cell. She'd also been helping her out with her investments, as well as a few other things. Nothing to do with the crime she'd not committed, but things like her home, her car, as well as money she got each month from her stocks. Without her helping, Parker would have been in serious trouble. No money, no home, and especially nothing to support herself while trying to find gainful employment—something she'd been told she had to do before she'd left the prison.

Walking to town was soothing to her body and mind. There were things she kept thinking about, like the list of shit she had to take care of because she'd been locked up for so long. Mostly little things, but there were other things too. Her craft, her father had called it, didn't have to be hidden away any longer. A lot of the magic she'd been gifted when her father was killed had grown with each day, it seemed to her.

Witchcraft had been in her family since well before even her father was born. Dad had told her it had been dwindling out, their magic because a lot of the older generations had married nonmagical people—just as his sister had done. But Parker seemed to have gotten the lion's share and then some, Dad had told her. Aunt Mae neither believed there was any magic to use nor that anyone in their family had ever practiced it. Aunt Mae was an idiot.

Her mother, a witch with hardly any magic, had been married off to her dad just so they could have her. It had never been a secret that her mother didn't love her dad. Parker thought she made up for it by loving her so much. Since she'd been born at home, everyone present knew Parker had more magic than her mother would ever have. As it turned out, more than her father did as well.

"Need a ride?" Shaking her head at the car moving along with her, the man laughed. "Come on, honey. You know you'll have a good time. I've been told you were just let out of prison. You have to be hard up for a real man between your legs."

She didn't have to ask him if it was her aunt who had told him to find her. Parker knew it for a fact that one or both of them had paid the man to come for her. The two men in the car smelled like her relatives. As she continued to walk, she snapped her fingers, and the man and his passenger swerved off the road and into a ditch. They'd not be killed, not if they stayed with their car. Lucky for them, the fresh air and the nice walk had put her in a wonderful and forgiving mood. Parker left them to their new dilemma as she reached out to her aunt and snapped her fingers again.

Having her aunt and uncle embarrassed was the best she could do without them being in front of her. Not that she couldn't do something from a distance, but she wanted to see them suffer — at least a little. When Parker dealt with her relatives, she wanted them to know who was turning their life upside down.

Besides, having her dress split up the back was no less than Aunt Mae deserved for wearing a dress two sizes too small. Her uncle was embarrassed too, but all she'd done to him was make sure he was present when Aunt Mae's dress fell to the floor. People shouldn't have to see that much flesh without it being a porn movie.

Reaching town at a reasonable hour, Parker found a restaurant and asked for a seat in the back. Her credit cards were still good, her credit rating better than it had been before she'd been put behind bars. Ordering herself a large diet cola as well as a large pizza, she looked around the room and the people there having dinner.

Much had changed while she'd been away, but most of it wasn't new to her. Mary had helped her keep up by bringing her magazines monthly, as well as a newspaper daily. It wasn't forbidden for her to do that for her, but it was sort of frowned upon. Parker owed Mary a great deal for her help. And she'd pay her back too.

As her pizza was set in front of her, a police officer sat too. He didn't take her pizza, which surprised her, but he did introduce himself by telling her his name. Captain Donny Franklin told her he'd heard she was headed this way.

"Do you have any plans of sticking around?" Parker told him she was only eating her dinner. "I'm not going to ask you to keep moving. I'm not even going to point out you should be with your aunt and uncle. If they were related to me, I'd have kept my distance from them too. Mary Cunningham is my cousin. She said you were an all right person."

"I have a home here. One that I owned before I was arrested." He said he knew that. That just today, he noticed it was being cleaned up and aired out. "I wasn't the one that killed my father."

"I know that. I knew that before you were taken away. But they don't ask cops what their opinion is before they arrest someone. I'm sorry you had to go through that. I knew your dad. He was a terrible man. I'm sorry if you think differently, but for some reason, I don't think you do." She nodded, putting down her slice of pizza. "Don't let me ruin your meal, Parker. I only came to sit with you because I'm aware of you and why you're here. There are a few things I want to talk to you about. But it's fine if we wait."

"I don't need a job. " Donny said he was all right with that, and he knew that she had some money. "Yes. Not as much as I'd like, but I can live off it for a while. Until I can get myself some income."

"There is a construction company here in town. It's been here for some time, but it's owned and operated by Brook and Ronan Foster. I think you know Ronan." Nodding, she told him that he was a year older than her. "I thought so. Mary said you should go and apply to work for them. Not that you're considered an ex-con, but Brook has a habit of hiring those sorts of people to help them get a foot into the working world. She's a good person too. We've never had any kind of trouble with their employees for as long as I've been an officer."

"Brook Garrett?" Donny said that was her. "I knew her parents. Not so much her. They were killed."

"Yes, both of them were by the same couple. The Quarters." Parker knew who they were as well. "They're both in prison and will be for a long time. Bethy is married now, with the cutest little boys I've ever seen. Twins. Married to a man whose name I can't remember right now. He's not been around here much so far as I know."

Parker didn't know why he was taking her down memory lane but let him talk. When offered a piece of her pizza, he took a slice. Parker ate with him. As he told her other tidbits she couldn't understand why he was sharing with her, she didn't pay much in the way of attention until he mentioned Carmilla Foster. Carmilla had helped her out a couple of times when she'd been hiding from her parents.

"She's living with her mother-in-law over by where Brook used to live with her family. All the Fosters live right around there. Do you remember them?" Telling him no seemed to make him have to tell her everything about them too. "Ronan has retired from the police force. He was going to be a part of our crew, but he's now the king of all lions. Pretty nice set up for them if you ask me. Don still teaches. He's really good at it too. My kids have been in his classes. They liked him. Quin is the town vet. It was a little touch and go there for a while whether or not he was going to find a place to open his practice, but he's got it going now. Cass is the attorney for the family. A good one too that you can depend on. Keegan, he's running some of the businesses for Brook and Ronan. I guess she's pretty wealthy. Then there is Loman. He's always been a loner and hasn't changed all that much. He's living here too when he's not out taking pictures of endangered animals or just things in general. What are you going to be doing, Parker?"

"I'll have to report to you because my relatives aren't going to help me." He said he'd figured that. It was another reason he'd come to sit with her. "You said you knew my dad. So you know about what I am."

"Yes. It's not common knowledge just so you're aware. I know, and a couple of the other cops know.

Mary told me. The others? I don't know how they found out. Your aunt and uncle, they don't know, do they?" Parker said she thought they didn't believe what she was. "Figures. They never mentioned it when they came by the office yesterday to tell me you were getting out. Since I already knew from Mary, I tuned them out when they were talking to the boss. I think they would have said something about you being a powerful witch. Don't you?"

"Yes. Anything to make me stand out." Donny asked her if she'd like to help him out when he needed it. "For solving crimes? I suppose. So long as you don't make a habit of it."

"I won't. I know you're a loner." When they polished off the rest of her pizza, he took the bill when it was laid on the table. "This was sort of a business meeting, so I'll pick up the tab. My wife, so you know, has been hired to work at your home. She's looking forward to getting to know you."

"I'm not good with people." Donny simply nodded. When Mary came in and joined them at the table, Parker had to breathe slowly so as not to overwhelm herself. She wasn't kidding when she told him she wasn't good with people. Parker didn't particularly like them at all. Especially when there were too many of them around her. "I have to go."

Neither of them stood when she did. Mary would know, and more than likely Donny too, that she'd been in confinement for six of the eight years she'd been locked up. Parker had to save Mary and a lot of other guards once, and that got her special treatment from a lot of the guards inside. She never had to share her space with anyone. Nor did she have to be outside when anyone else was. It would have been dangerous to the others. Not her—she was too strong to be caught off guard—but from anyone gunning for her to take what her father had wanted from her that day. That was what made her a danger to herself. People would get themselves dead if they tried anything with her.

Parker made her way to her home. There didn't seem to be anyone there, as all the lights were off, so she let herself in via the back door and made her way up to what had always been her bedroom. The master suite was the perfect size for her to spread out should she need to when casting spells or practicing.

There was a note on the bathroom vanity. Picking it up, she read who was going to be working in the house with her as well as what her job was. She supposed Mary had made sure she had this note. Parker could only hope that Judith Franklin was going to be all right with a witch in the house. The name would also keep her from having to fumble around for a name when she met her.

Parker couldn't make herself relax enough to sleep. Pulling the sheet off the bed, she dragged it and her pillow out to the wrap around second story deck and laid out there on a lounger. The slight breeze and the sounds that only living in the country could bring a person helped her to fall asleep.

~~~

Don was happy for the summer months. Not that he changed up his schedule all that much when he didn't have classes. He still rose at the same time and went to bed when it was barely dark out. However, tonight he was having some trouble relaxing enough to make himself sleep.

Shifting into his lion, he roamed around in the fields behind the houses along the area he lived in. He knew if one of his brothers were out and about, they'd join him. Don would be just as happy if they were all cozy in their beds and left him to his own.

Not that he didn't love his family, but today had been a particularly long day, one that had him spending too much time behind four walls and doing things he wished he'd just done at home. Shopping for furniture wasn't exactly how he wanted to spend a lovely June day.

The worst part about the day from hell, he'd dubbed it, was that he'd not found a single stick of furniture to go in his home. Nothing suited him—it was all chrome and glass, nothing wooden or smooth. That was another thing he couldn't understand. Why did everything have to have texture to it? Why not just leave wood alone?

Of course, he'd not put that question to anyone. He didn't want to seem stupid, and he thought if word got around of his query and his mother and grandma found out, they would murder him. Smiling to himself, Don lifted his overly sensitive nose to the air and inhaled deeply.

Someone was close. Not only that, but he could smell blood. Lying down in the soft grass with his head only inches above the highest reeds, he looked around for the source of the scent. It wasn't until he saw her, the woman standing in the moonlight, that he realized someone besides his family had access to the wooded area behind their homes.

Don didn't want anyone around that he didn't know. Nor did he want someone around that would harm one of the kids that might be hanging around. His plan, if he really wanted to call it that, was to sneak up to her and scare her—just a little. But almost as soon as he moved again, she turned around and looked directly at him.

Don't move.

He didn't. Don's paw was up, his tail curled next to his body. It took him a full minute to realize she'd just told him not to move. Him? A lion? Wasn't she scared of him? Or at least impressed or something?

When she put her finger to her lips then pointed, he looked in that direction. *There are two men beyond here that have no right to be on the land back here. I can smell the fresh blood. I'm assuming that's what brought you to me.* Don kept an eye on the men he could see now and spoke to the woman in the same way she'd done for him.

Is it a human that is bleeding? She told him it was a

deer. They had been night hunting with goggles on. *This is private land. Did you know that when you came out here?*

Yes. Nothing more. Nothing to say she was sorry, nor did she make excuses for why she was out here too. *I'm going to give them a scare. You could, I suppose, but if you show yourself, everyone in the territory will be out looking for a large cat. It won't even matter to them if they happen to kill a house cat.*

Don watched her move. She wasn't touching the earth. Not a single blade of grass bent under her feet. The branches surrounding her didn't snap or make a sound when she moved over them. So caught up on watching her, he nearly leapt up to take the men down when they began to scream bloody murder about something hurting them.

The two men nearly ran over him in their haste to get away. Moving quickly, Don barely managed to get out of the way of their feet when they kept knocking each other over. Every time one of them would fall, they'd scream about something grabbing their legs. Don didn't see anything that looked as if it was touching them. However, they were running through the brambles.

After they were out of sight, Don looked for the woman again. She was far enough away from him now that he knew he'd have to run to catch up to her. Not knowing a thing about her, not her name or even her scent, he only just realized he was going to be at a loss to ask her what she'd done to the men. As he hunted for her scent in the area where he'd seen her, he noted to himself that there was nothing of her anywhere. Looking for her again, he noticed that she'd disappeared as if she'd never been with him at all.

Perplexed, he made his way back to his home. The waterway that ran directly behind his home was the first place he stopped by as he walked. The night moon was bright with light, but he couldn't see where the woman had gone. Moving his now exhausted body up onto his deck, Don reached out for her. She'd spoken to him, so he thought he should be able to speak to her too.

I'm not much of a people person. He thought that was an odd way of answering his call. *I'm also not human.*

Neither am I, as you well know. Where do you live? After asking, he knew it was a long shot if she told him that kind of personal information. *I live in this cul-de-sac with the rest of my family. Why are you roaming around here in the middle of the night?* Another dumb question, but he was glad he asked when she laughed.

I was having trouble sleeping. The same as you. Why do any of these things you're asking me matter to you? I've not intruded on your personal life. How about you do the same for me? He didn't have an answer to that. Don thought that telling her he wanted to meet her face to face would get him killed. *I don't murder people for being curious, Mr. Foster. I'm a better person than that.*

He'd hurt her. Don wasn't sure how he'd done it, but he knew he had. *I'm sorry. I didn't mean to come across —*

You know my name. Her laughter again. *You have a lovely laugh. It reminds me of summer. How that connection was made, I haven't any idea. But that's what I feel when you do it. Also, I have no idea why, but I don't think you've had much of an occasion to laugh as late.*

That is about as close to the truth as you could ever be. However, you're inevitably going to hear about me, so believe what you wish of whatever you hear. I was only just released from prison today. My name is Parker Carter. I was wrongly accused of killing my father. I live on the next street over from where you are now. He wondered why she'd been in prison and for how long. *If you have questions, Mr. Foster, ask them. I'm not in the mood to sugarcoat the answers. Actually, I'm rarely in the mood to do that. I know your mother. She saved me a few times when my father was out looking for me.*

I'd rather hear information from you if you don't mind. I don't know why, but it seems important to me that I hear the truth, and not someone else's version of what they think has happened. She thanked him. For whatever reason, Don thought she didn't quite believe him. *Why do I have the feeling that the two of us are going to be good friends, Parker?*

Because, Lionheart, I'm your mate.

When the connection between them closed, he didn't move off the deck until the sun was coming up over the forest of trees behind his home. If asked, Don wasn't sure he could have put his finger on a single thought that had been roaming around in his head.

Parker was his mate? She knew his mother. Don

shifted back to his other side and went into the house. It was time, he thought, for him to speak to his mom. Other than Parker, he knew she might be the only one that would make sure he had the truth as much as Parker would have told him. She was his mate?

Chapter 2

Don was waiting on the back deck when he heard his mom and grandma in the kitchen. Knocking once on the door, he left himself in. It had always been wonderful to know he could count on his mom having her doors unlocked. Now that Rollin, his father, was history, she seemed to be a great deal more relaxed too.

"Hello, son. My, you're up early. I don't even have water on for the tea yet." He told her he could eat if she was going to be cooking. "Of course. I was going to make pancakes, but Jane is insisting on waffles with cinnamon bits in them."

"I can eat either of those. Or both if you're going to end up doing that." She glared at him a little, and Don winked at his grandma. "You know you don't mind having your son around to cook for. I'll even tell you what I figured out last night. Well, I didn't actually do the figuring. But I have some news. Do you know Parker

Carter?"

The bowl in his mom's hands shattered on the floor when she dropped it. Thinking to tease her, he didn't when he had a look at her face. Guiding her to the chair, he sat her down and got her a glass of water. Whatever had happened between her and Parker really shook her up.

"Where is she?" Don told his mom what he knew, which really wasn't all that much. He didn't, however, tell her she was his mate. Mom was just too shaken right now. "That poor child. I used to hide her away when she was younger. Her parents would be looking for her all over town, and I flat out lied to them every time they checked to see if she was here with me."

"She told me she's only just been released from prison. Yesterday, as a matter of fact. Something about the death of her father." Mom got up and moved to the cabinets as he cleaned up the broken glass. "There were a couple of hunters on our land last night while I was out as my cat. I think she might have saved me from getting shot by running them off. Did you know she was a witch?"

"I did." She handed him a large poster book, the kind that used to be kept around for newspaper articles and such. This one was filled with articles, all right. It seemed they were all about Parker. "The first time I saw her, she was a dirty little thing. Told me that her mom was mad at her for casting in the house. I didn't understand that until later. But once I got her cleaned up a little and had her put on one of you boys' old shirts, she told me a great deal. I never believed she killed her father. Even though he should have been put down a long time ago if you ask me."

"I've not seen her as yet. Nor gotten close enough to her to figure out if what she told me last night was true. Parker said I was her mate." Mom sat back down again, and Grandma yelled at her for being a jack in the box. "She lives in one of the houses behind mine, she said. Parker also told me I shouldn't believe everything I've heard about her. But she did know you, and I thought you'd help me out. Is she something I'm going to regret being mated to, Mom?"

"I wouldn't think so. She's beautiful. Tall, I remember thinking when she was a child. How did you not get close enough to her to catch her scent when she knew?" Don told his mom he didn't know. "I'd believe her, Don. But I do want to let you know, Parker is a little bit on the rough side. If you think Brook had a hard life, wait until you hear about Parker's. That poor child. She has some relatives around too. Uncle and an aunt if I remember correctly."

"She didn't mention them." Mom got up to begin making breakfast. "I was going to go and see her today. I'm not sure if I want to or not, but I think I should."

"You should. Better yet, you should just go there now and have her come here for something to eat with us. I'd love to see and talk to her again." He said he didn't know where she lived. He also told her they had a connection. "I would imagine we all have one with her. She was working hard at being a strong witch even when she was just a teenager. I wonder how that went over in prison for her."

After telling his mom he didn't know, he went to the living room to contact Parker. That way, if she yelled at him or even turned him into something, he'd be able to beg her to not hurt him without his mom and grandma around.

You do have some strange thoughts, don't you? Don grinned and told her she was just the person he wanted to speak to. *So I felt. I have no desire at all to turn anyone into anything today. I've just been notified that along with my early release because someone finally got their head out of their asses, I've also been given a check for my time served. What the hell am I supposed to do with this?*

Cashing it comes to mind. She told him she didn't have any accounts. *I do. My mom wants to see you, anyway. If you let me pick you up and take you to the bank, then here, I'll help you set it up. Mom did remember you, all right. Also, she wants to make you breakfast. I want to come and get you to bring you here.*

I don't do people well, Don. He said they'd not crowd her. *What I mean is, I'm not in the mood to be looked at like a bug under a microscope. Please tell your mom that —*

She's not going to be happy. I'm actually wondering why she's not just gone to each of the houses where you told me you lived and started knocking on doors. You'd save your neighbors a great deal of embarrassment if you just let me get you and bring you here. She didn't say anything, and he was worried she really didn't want to come over. *Please?*

This is a really bad idea. I heard you were a teacher, Don. What do you think the board is going to say when they figure out you're mated to an ex-con? He told her he didn't care and pointed out she wasn't an ex anything. *People only hear and see what they want. In this case, they're going to hear I was in prison and nothing more.*

That much he knew to be true. People did have a tendency to only hear or see what they wanted. Even as a teacher, he could see that in the kids' parents when they came in for teacher conferences.

Parker, I'm going to get into my car now and drive up and down your street until you come out and get into my car. He told her what it looked like. *You know my name. While I know nothing about you other than your name, I'm going to be yelling it out my window the entire time I'm waiting on you to come out and get into my car.*

Parker told him she'd be out front, but not to expect much. He hadn't any idea what she might have meant by that, so he ignored it — for now, at least. Telling his mom and Grandma he was going to get Parker, he kissed both of them on the cheeks and left. Don was really happy he'd not had to yell for her. He wasn't sure how he'd ever live that down once his brothers heard about it.

Just as she said she'd be, Parker was sitting on the

front porch of her home. He didn't get a good look at her last night, so was surprised by her beauty. As she made her way down the short walk to his car, Don realized his mother had been wrong about Parker. She wasn't beautiful but gorgeous — and tall. He'd bet if they stood toe to toe, she'd only be a few inches shorter than he was. Once she was in the car and buckled, all Don wanted to do was look at her. Christ, he belonged to a beauty queen.

"Just drive, moron." He laughed as he pulled into her drive to turn around. "I've been thinking about a few things you should know. I mean, if this goes anywhere, you're going to have to be prepared for whatever shit hits the fan. My mom, she's still alive. I haven't spoken to her in years. For some reason, she'd send me things while I was in prison, but she rarely came to see me. I was told she wasn't doing it to hurt me. I'm not sure what to think about it, however. We were always very close, the two of us."

"I'm close to my mom. All of us are. There are six of us, by the way. My dad, I don't know if you remember him or not, but he was a real shit." Parker told him she didn't remember him all that much. "Lucky you. My grandma is living with my mom. Or the other way around. I'm not sure who is living with whom. But they're incredibly happy, the two of them. I came by to see my mom this morning to tell her you were around."

"She told you to leave me where I was, didn't she?"

Don told her what his mom had said about her coming to breakfast. "I wasn't kidding when I said I'm not good around people, Don. Crowds of them, even if there are only three or four, make me want to curl into a ball and shut them all out. I've been alone most of my adult life."

"I didn't invite my brothers over to meet you just yet. I promise to let them know not to crowd you. We'll get through this." She didn't say anything as he pulled into his mom's drive. Sitting in the car with Parker, he wasn't sure what to do when he saw that two of his brothers were there already. "I'm going to take you back home. My brothers are already here. If I know them, they already know that I belong to you. That will make them stick around just so they can meet you. I'm sorry."

She didn't say anything when she opened the car door and got out. Joining her on the front lawn, he told her that at any time they could leave the house. She only had to say the word. Instead of going inside, she turned and looked at him.

"This will be hard on me; I'm not going to lie to you. But I'm going to have to get used to them at some point. If they get out of hand or piss me off in some way, I can just make them quiet." He wasn't sure that was going to go over well either or said that to her. "Then we'd better hope for the best, right?"

She was in the house when he realized she'd left him out there, more than likely with his mouth hanging open. As soon as he entered the house, he knew this wasn't going to end well for any of the rest of his family. Brook was already yelling about something, and he heard one of the babies crying. That meant Bethy was there as well. This wasn't going to be good. Not one bit, Don thought.

As he entered the kitchen where they all seemed to be congregated, he found Jasper feeding one of the boys a bottle. Asking where everyone was, he pointed to the dining room and said they were having some cereal for their first meal of the day. Jasper laughed when he asked where his mate was.

"I didn't know you had one. When did this—?"

The way Jasper stood up, bottle and baby forgotten in his hands, Don felt his cat run over his skin. The need to shift was great. Looking behind him to see what had Jasper so upset, he saw that Parker was looking at Jasper in much the same way as if being in the same room together was going to cause some sort of interstellar explosion at any second.

"Parker."

Don moved out of the way when Parker came more into the room with them. Parker took the baby from Jasper and handed it off to him. Don didn't dare take his eyes off the two people in front of him, but he did worry for the baby's safety. As soon as his mom came in, Don handed Joey, he thought he had, to her. Whatever happened next, he wanted to have both his hands free to help with it.

The slap to Jasper's face brought his cat to the front of

him. A second slap had his lion curling back away from what his mate was doing to the incredibly old fae. When she drew back to no doubt hit him again, Jasper grabbed her hand.

"You've made your point, my lady." Parker was freed from his hand, but neither of them looked at all happy with each other. Then Jasper, still staring at Parker, started speaking. "I had no idea until you were being released that you had been arrested. If you remember, your father did a great deal of damage to me that day."

"It's too bad he didn't kill you as well." Parker started to cry and shook her head. "I didn't mean that. You saved my life that day. I can never thank you enough for what you did. Even spending all that time in prison, I knew it was because I was safe from him forever."

"You killed her father." Jasper and Parker looked at him as if they only just remembered he was there. "I'm sorry. But you were the one that killed her father, and she went to prison for it."

"Her father decided he was going to kill Parker for her magic. Little did he know, her death would have been his death too. Not because she would have killed him, but because he'd not have been able to handle the power his daughter had accumulated. She's much more powerful than any other witch I've ever come across."

~~~

Parker didn't want to sit and eat with the family. It wasn't because she was overwhelmed, but because

there were too many people at the table that brought
memories she wasn't ready to deal with today. If ever.
When Carmilla said her name, she looked at the woman
who, like Jasper, had saved her life.

"You might feel a good deal better, honey, if you were
to tell us what happened that day. We know he killed your
father, but nothing more than that. The papers didn't say
anything about how he was killed." She looked at Jasper,
then at Don when he took her hand. "They will never
judge you for whatever happened that day. You're here
with us because of what Jasper did for you."

"His head was removed." No one at the table spoke
when she did. It was like the mute button had been
pushed just for her to be heard. "My father, he'd been
training me since I was born. For what, I was never sure.
Magic just seemed to come naturally to me. To be honest,
my power had always been there for me to use, and I
knew how to use it. Jasper was there for me, as well.
He had been since birth, I think. Then my father started
training me for other things after I turned thirteen—
black magic, I saw. It was...without Jasper being there for
me, my dad might well have trained me to be something
entirely different."

"Park, her father, saw she was powerful from the
beginning, I think. Her birth drew me to her because of
the amount of power she had from birth. I watched over
her from a distance at first." Jasper lifted his hand up and
showed her, in a hologram sort of picture, what she had

been doing when he'd watched her. He continued telling his part of the story. "There wasn't any need for them to care for her as an infant. As you can see, she was able to care for herself, meet her own needs, even before they noticed the strength she had."

She was taking a bottle at one point, then changed her own diaper. Her clothing changed, as well. There was never any need for anything else in the room, but it was there, she could see. Jasper went on to say how she, even as an infant, was ignored by the world, including her father, until she was older. Her mom, Jasper said, was a good person, kind and loving to her child.

"I would check on her. Not as much as I should have, I realize now. She was taking such good care of herself, I slipped up and didn't see her again until she was about eight." Parker told him she'd just turned eight, so he was right. "It was then I noticed she was being groomed for darker magic. It bothered her. That, I realized, was what brought me back to her side. At night I'd go to her room and untrain her on the magic her father was teaching her. I tried to turn Park from what he was doing, but he wouldn't have it. I think to this day, there were stronger forces with him, telling him to train her the way he was."

"There was a man there—I would see him at times when they were talking to him. He wanted me to do things for him. I think it was his plan to take me from my parents to have me work for him. Even at a young age, I knew he was dangerous." Don asked her what had happened to him. "He's dead."

When no one asked her how he'd come to be in such a permanent state, she didn't bother to explain to them. She'd done it, killed him when he'd snuck into the house and taken her from her bed. Parker had known somehow that screaming wouldn't have brought her parents to her, so she killed him quickly and sent his body away. Parker wondered if anyone had ever found his body in the wooded area around the park where he lived.

"Parker?" She looked at Don when he said her name, then around the table. "Jasper said you were to tell us the rest. This was your story."

"You mean me calling for him? I didn't. Jasper had helped me a great deal, you see. And we could communicate much like you and I can. However, it was more than that when I was taken. Jasper felt my terror." Don asked her if she'd saved him. With a short nod from Jasper, she nodded that she had. "He wasn't caught at our home, but he had been caught by someone. They were going to murder him for a crime he didn't commit. Or at least I didn't think he'd committed. There were other forces around that had wanted me, you see. They thought to get me through him by having him suffer in a jail cell without windows or any way for him to survive. Jasper needs the outdoors as much as we do air in our lungs. To kill a witch, even as a child as strong as I was, would have netted someone a great coup. So I helped him escape from them as they were ready to chain him in iron."

"It would have killed me with only that. But as Parker said, the windowless cell, along with no way to feed myself on the perfume of flowers and trees, would have eventually killed me." Don asked if he would have given her up. "Never. I would have gladly died for her to live. I still would. But that is, thankfully, not going to be a problem ever again."

"Why?" Parker asked Jane what she meant. "Why will you not have a problem with dying? I'm assuming you have some kind of power with being mated now. Is that it?"

Parker looked at each of the people in the room with her. Did they not know? How could they not have been told they were all immortals because of what Ronan was? She looked at Jasper when he laughed.

"I believe they've been hoodwinked, my lady. I cannot find in any of their minds that they were told of this." Jane asked again what was going on. "You're immortal. Nothing that either I or Parker have given you, but either of us would have if you'd not had it already. You've had it for a while now, at least since Ronan became king of the lions. None of you can be harmed or killed. You cannot be taken to be used against him to change a law or a ruling. With Ronan—and by being his mate, Brook— you all were made to be immortal."

"Wait. Wait a minute here. I don't want to be immortal." Jane looked at Parker and looked ready to cry. "I'm an old woman already, child. I ache at times so badly that I have no desire to get up from my bed. Even to move around in my own home sometimes is too much for these old bones. It's why I never shift any longer. It's just too painful."

Parker put her hand out before speaking. "I can take it all away from you if you wish. The choice is yours. I can also take the pain away—all of it. You won't be any younger, I'm sorry about that. But I can either make it so you die someday or give you magic that would heal you. Not only the aches and pains of age but also the ache you have deep in your heart. The pain that keeps you up at night."

Jane looked at her for several seconds before she took her hand into hers. "I would like to not ache anymore, my child. But—and I'm not pressuring you at all—but I would very much like to have a purpose. Something that I can do to make a difference in not just my life, but those here and beyond. If you could do that for me, then I'd live—"

"You don't think you have a purpose? You think that we, as your family, don't think it's worth having you around?" Parker gave her some of her memories of the boys, as they called them, going to her for advice. "This is only but in a single day, Jane. Everyone, including Ronan, the king of your kind, comes to you for not just guidance, but also love and support. You must know that the love these people have for you would only grow exponentially even if you were to choose death."

"You too, Parker? Do you want me around? I have no idea why that's important to me, but it is. I'd like for you to think of me as your grandma, as they do. I'd like it if both you and Brook think of me as more than just an in-law that is old and cranky." Brook spoke up from the doorway she'd been standing in with Ronan for several minutes. "I need to know that I'm not a burden on anyone."

Parker rarely looked into the future. She could, for centuries ahead. But all she gave Jane was a small part of what the future held for her. Jane helped in the birth of Brook's child, saving not just the child's life, but Brook's as well. For without Jane, the child would not survive complications at birth, and it would hurt Brook enough that she would go to Jasper to take away her immortality so she could go with her son.

Jane nodded. When Parker took a glimpse into the future away, tucking it away for later, she asked her again what she wanted from her. When there was no answer forthcoming, Parker smiled at her.

"Grandma, would you like to be around forever with your family? A family that will grow and learn at your feet. A group that has never thought anything of you but love and kindness. You have no reason to think it was your fault that Rollin was such a person. You know why he was like he was. There is no blame for you in all that he did." Jane said he had learned it from his father. "Yes.

And it didn't matter that you tried your best to change his mind about hitting people, stealing what he didn't have or need. You aren't to feel guilty for someone else having to take his life, either. Brook would have done it over and over just to have you here with us."

"I would have. I told you that." Jane leaned her head on Brook's shoulder when she sat next to her. "I'm telling you right now, if you choose death after being given this gift, I will beat you stupid. I swear, I'm not going to let you leave me when I've only just fallen in love with having you around."

"I want to live." Parker let go of the magic that was at her fingertips. There had been extensive damage done to Jane's body because of her son and husband. When Jane stiffened her body as hard as the iron particles that were racing through her bloodstream again because of her son and husband, Parker took it into herself and destroyed it. "Oh, my goodness. I can feel it."

No one moved when Jane stood up. She smiled, then laughed. As she grabbed her grandson Ronan, the two of them danced around the dining room as if they were in a grand ballroom all by themselves. Each one of the grandsons took their turn, giving her a twirl around the large room as the rest of them laughed.

When they were all seated except for Jane, she came to Parker and pulled her up from the chair. The hug that she gave her was tight, loving, and didn't bring out any of the feelings she generally had with being touched.

Returning the hug to her, Parker could feel that not only was Jane happy with being without pain, but she was also happy just to be alive. Also, being here with the family she loved more than she did her own self.

They were still sitting there well into the lunch hour. Questions were shot out like a scattergun on a turkey shoot. Answers were a little long in coming. Brook, Parker realized, was much like she was—ask me your questions, but be assured you might well not like the answers. As they migrated to the living room, a room that was as welcoming as the dining room had been, they stretched out and continued speaking of whatever entered their minds.

"I have a question for you and Jasper." Jasper's wife, a tiny little thing, sat down next to her when Don got up to get drinks brought in for the rest of them. "You've been in jail. I'm sorry for that. But how did no one notice how much magic you had? I mean, I can feel it like it's something warm to me. Wouldn't others have felt it as well?"

"Only other shifters." She said she was human. "You've not been human since you found Jasper was your mate. Don't you people take stock in yourselves? You all should have realized what you were the moment it happened to you. Not to mention, being able to heal each other by magic."

She was laughing until Jasper stood up. His other self, his fae counterpart, came out, and it was a beautiful sight. His wings, as old as time, were opened behind him, long and touching the floor. He didn't say a word as his body took the shape of the fae he was. Anyone in the room would have been impressed as much as she was if there wasn't a sense of danger in all of them.

"She's back." Jasper looked at her, then repeated himself. "Your mother. She's back. Judith heard you were released and has come to bargain with you—or just to talk to you. I can't find a stable answer from her. Her mind seems to be more chaotic than I remember."

"Does she know where I am?" Jasper closed his eyes as his fae turned back to himself. The thought of danger, Parker thought, was what had brought him out. When he nodded, she looked around the room. "My mother isn't insane. I don't mean that she's not having an issue right now, but there is something very wrong with her. I don't know how she was able to free herself from the hospital she was in, but she's dangerous, I was told. I don't know how much of that I believe, to be honest. This is so out of character for her that I'm having a hard time equating the information I've been given to the woman who raised me."

"How long has she been locked up?" Parker had to think. When she gave them the answer, Ronan sat down. "That's the same amount of time you were away. Is there a correlation between the dates? I mean, did something happen, other than your father being killed, that would have done this to her?"

"I wouldn't have thought so. She apparently thinks I'm out to get her since I was accused of taking out my father. I didn't. Nor do I want to harm her in any way. But if she comes here, thinking to harm any of us in any way, I'll— Actually, I think it would be better if I were just to talk to her. To see what she has to say about all this." Ronan looked at Don, then back at her. "She'll be all right. As I said, I don't want to hurt her, and I won't, but I won't allow her to hurt any of you guys either."

"Then we'll have to be ready for her." He stood up, Don and the others following suit. "We're all family here. She'd better realize we'll stop at nothing to keep you safe too."

Parker wondered if he realized she couldn't harm her mom any more than she could Don if he were in the same condition—a little off, and very confusing to be around. Mother would give a hug to a person she didn't know. Parker didn't know how to react to the person her mother had become, someone that needed to be hospitalized. Whatever happened now, she would try and work with the others. If they didn't want to do things her way, she'd do it on her own. Parker had much more experience than they did in dealing with her mom. But with this person, Parker didn't know if she should be better prepared for the unknown.

Chapter 3

Don didn't know what to do with himself. He had a mate, but he didn't want her to think he was going to jump her every time she was close. He wanted to, more than he did anything else in his head right now. But she was still a little gun shy. Not to mention, he could tell she was upset. It hurt him in ways he couldn't nail down. Her pain was his pain. Don could do nothing to help her with it.

"There is something I need for you to know." She'd come into his office a few minutes ago and not said a word. Parker sat in the chair across from the only other place to sit in here. Don asked her what she needed to tell him. "First of all, can you try and cast? I'm not sure how you smell to me." She laughed when he cocked his brow at her. "What I mean is, you don't smell any different than you did the first time I saw you face to face. You might have taken on a part of me then. I have no idea how to tell if you've received some or all of my magic."

"I haven't any idea how to cast things, Parker. Expect to toss trash out. If that's what you mean, I'm exceptionally good at tossing things away that have no meaning to me." She told him it wasn't what she meant. "No, I didn't think so. Tell me how to do it, and I'm game. I was just sitting here thinking how bored I am. Do you want to live here with me?"

"Yes. But I have things at my home that I'd like to blend in with your things. You don't have much, do you?" He told her why. "I can understand that, as well. But we don't need to go anywhere to shop. At least I don't. We'll get to that in a second. I want you to think of the pillow on the chair in the living room. It's the only one in there, so you should be able to remember it, correct?"

"Yes. I think it's ugly." Laughing, she told him she thought so as well. "All right. I have an image of it in my mind. Now what?"

"Okay. Tricky part now. Don't think of bringing it to you, but that it's right here on the desk." When she laughed, he opened his eyes. He'd not thought of them being closed, but her laughter made him feel good. The pillow, the ugliest one he'd ever laid eyes on, was on his desk. "You can do it. Easily too, it looked like."

"Honestly, I only thought of tossing it out." She laughed again, telling him to try something else. "What? I don't know what I can do. This is sort of fun. Something I never thought I'd be able to say about magic. I lived a very sheltered life until I found you in the woods."

"That was extremely sweet of you. Okay. This magic is something that came with Ronan being king. You can think of clothing and it will appear on you. I have no idea why I think this is funny, but it might be kinda fun to know more than your brother about shit like this."

He thought of a pair of shorts he'd seen online a while ago. The fit of them was perfect on his body even though he'd not thought of that. Asking Parker about it, she nodded.

"Since it's for you to wear, it would be only for you. Even if you were to take it off at some point, it would only ever fit you."

He liked that idea. The more the two of them thought of things he could do, the louder their laughter got. It was fun, he thought, to do things he'd never even imagined before. As they made their way to the empty rooms in the house, he had an idea about what he'd like to see in the dining room. Before either of them stepped into the smallish room, it was twice the size it had been, with a beautiful long wooden table taking up most all the space in the middle of the room. The chairs surrounding it were a perfect match for the idea he'd had in his head.

"I love this." He nodded when Parker ran her hand down the length of the table. "There needs to be more room in here. We'll need to have a bit of space for corner cabinets for dishes and linens. This room couldn't hold all your family, especially if the others find their mates too."

Corner cabinets appeared, then disappeared in the corners. Even as he was wondering what he'd done wrong, another set, this one much larger, was set in the spaces along with the room getting exponentially bigger. Don looked at Parker when she laughed again.

"These were at my house. I don't remember where they came from. They might well have been a part of the house. But I think they're a perfect match to this room. I love how you put in windows too. It will make the room look larger, though it is pretty big now." Don went to the window that looked out over the back yard. As he stood there, the window lengthened until it touched the floor. Then it changed into a patio door that would slide open to the decking that was currently being built. "This is about as freaky as I've ever witnessed. Usually, I would think of something while I was away from the house or whatever I wanted to change. It would be done without me seeing it. But this, this is amazing. You have excellent taste in the way things should be. I'm betting it has something to do with you being a teacher. You'd have to be pretty organized for that sort of job."

"I am that way in my classroom. I want to be able to just pick things up at a moment's notice without fumbling around for it. However, you'll see that my closet and my room are a disaster. Like a tornado went through there and left behind a mess." She told him from now on he could easily have it cleaned as soon as he left the room.

"I'll have to think on that one. It would really give me the willies if I came into the room while it was cleaning up after me."

"I think you might be right on that. You can, if you wish, have things just the way they are until you leave the house. I think I might have that in any of the rooms I'm in. I don't mind the changes. I just don't think I want to be in the way if one of the things happens where I'm standing." Don laughed with her. It was the most fun he'd had in a long while—even more than he'd had at school. "I've been thinking about my mother since Jasper told us she was here. I think I'd like to speak to her about some things. I wonder if that would be possible to have a conversation with her."

"You do whatever you think you need to do. However, I would only request that you take me with you. I don't know what sort of help I could be for you, but I'd feel better if you didn't go to see her alone." She nodded and entered the living room ahead of him. "What is it, Parker? You seem upset now. We were having so much fun before."

"I'm still having fun. I was just thinking about her, and I wonder what happened that would have made her go off the edge like she did. Something is bothering her. I want to find out what it is." Don didn't know anything about her parents, so he didn't have any answers for her. "I would like to change this room around completely if you don't mind. I love the way the fireplace is there between the bookshelves, but I don't care for the way the other windows are so small. I'm a person who loves to have the outdoors around me as much as I possibly can."

He agreed with her, but he was still sorry that her mom had intruded on their fun. Looking around the room, Don thought of the most outrageous things he could think of as their furniture. They both burst out laughing as the room moved around at dizzying speeds.

"I do hope you're having fun with me." He was laughing so hard all he could do was hang onto the green and pink couch and laugh harder. "Christ, would you look at those bookshelves? Is that concrete bricks on display there? What is up with that rug? Don, it's moving. And the artwork on the walls looks like someone puked on a canvas."

Everything she pointed out to him made him laugh all the harder. It was hurting him to stand up like he was, so he laid down. As soon as his back touched the couch, he nearly pissed himself when a large piece of burlap wrapped around his body. This was too much. Even when he closed his eyes, the room was still burnt into his memory. Redecorating had never been this fun before.

When he opened his eyes, he could see that she'd taken his fun away and replaced it with much more muted colors. The couch was now a soft brown. The curtains, black and some kind of yellowy pus color, were just gone. The room was just the way he might have picked out if he'd seen it in a shop. Getting up, he even liked the coffee table/footstool.

The earth tone colors made his entire body relax. His mind slowed down. The picture over the fireplace was one that he was sure his brother had taken, of a lioness and her cubs. Walking to it, he could see Loman's signature in the corner, a small paw print that was on all his photos.

"I saw it in your mind. I hope you don't mind." He said he had always loved this picture Loman had taken. "I do, as well. He must have been close to her and her cubs for him to get a shot like this. There are others I'd love to have in this room. Do you think he'd mind?"

"No. He's forever showing us his pictures. This is, I must admit, the first one I've seen blown up like this. It shows a great deal of the detail I'm sure he's famous for." Parker said Loman was incredibly famous. "He is. I know he is. However, to hear him talking about himself, you'd think he has to work hard to have people want to put his photos in a magazine. This one has always been my favorite of all his pictures."

It took them the rest of the day to get the house in order. Parker decided to sell her home — she'd not lived in it for a long time anyway. Also, she had a cook and mentioned that they could bring Mrs. Franklin here if she wished. Parker assured him that Mrs. Franklin was a fantastic cook.

"We never spoke about money." He told her he only had this house because of Brook. "She's a nice person. A little intense, but I like her. I have some. I mean, I have stocks in a lot of companies: some personal property, but nothing in cash. I had to keep switching it around so my relatives wouldn't pounce on it. My aunt thought I should have lost everything when I supposedly killed my father. At first, there was money in my account, but when I figured out she was simply taking it, I stopped putting money in it. Mary, the guard, is a friend of mine. She helped me invest it when I asked her to."

"I'm a teacher and have the low pay that goes with being one. I do love my job, however. The money was good enough for me to put a little aside to send Mom each payday and for me to pay my rent. I also had a few part-time jobs that helped me make my rent and eat in the summer months. Like right now, I have less than twenty bucks in my checking account. I do have the money my grandma gave me, but I haven't done anything with it as yet." He laughed. "To be honest, I've never looked in the envelope since I got it. I haven't any idea how much money she gave me."

On the search to find the envelope, Don realized how much they'd gotten done today. Not only did the house feel like a home now, but it was filled out in ways he'd never imagined it would have been. Even going into the kitchen didn't seem like he needed to avoid it anymore. The things they'd chosen to have in their home, he thought, reflected both their tastes. He thought that was the way it should have been from the start.

There was fifty grand in the envelope, along with a key to a safety deposit box. While he had no idea what was in it, he was satisfied with what had been in his part of his grandma's estate.

"She wanted to see us having fun with the money before she died. That's not going to happen now. So I wonder, should I give it back to her? I mean, it's a great deal of cash, and she might need it while living forever." Parker sat down across from him and handed him half her sandwich. While she told him she couldn't cook at all, her sandwich looked incredibly good. "I don't want to hurt her feelings by asking her, however."

"Your grandma and mom are going to be fine. Both with money as well as living around here with all you guys close by." Parker took a bite of her sandwich and moaned. Don nearly dropped his sandwich when she did that. "You're not eating. What's wrong?"

"You. You moaned." She nodded, then her face turned a bright shade of red. "Yes. I can see you've gotten it. I'm trying my best to not leap on you whenever I'm close, but hearing you moan nearly made me come in my brand new shorts."

"Well, we can't have that happen. They are brand new." She put the rest of her sandwich on the paper plate she'd gotten for them. "I don't like sex. I mean, I've had it before. But it didn't really do anything for me. I suppose it could have been the person I was with. He did tell me he was good at it." She laughed.

"I'm going to enjoy making love with you." She looked at him, and he felt his cock stretch even more. His body, even his cat, responded to her when she moved on the chair. "We have a bed now. We could if you'd like, go up and break it in."

"You're such a romantic. Has anyone ever told you that before?" He shook his head. "Good answer. I'll race you to the bed."

Then, just like that, Don fell in love with his mate. He'd have told her that, too, if she'd been there. But the moment she said she'd race him, she disappeared. That was a trick, he thought, he'd better learn first. He'd hate to make her wait too long for him to get to their bedroom.

~~~

The bedroom had been one of the first things they'd played around with. It was nothing like the rest of the house. This room was neither warm nor inviting. There was color if you counted beige and white as colors. They were, she knew, but they just weren't restful colors in a room she hoped to sleep well in. Something she'd not been able to do in some time, honestly.

Without changing out the blocky furniture she didn't care for, Parker made the room warm by adding splashes of color. The bedspread was now a quilt. The colors of the blocks were now all over the room. Even the blinds — no curtains for this room — weren't white any longer, but a beautiful shade of blue, a color she loved over most anything else.

The floors were hardwood. While she didn't mind the wood around the house, the bedroom needed softness. The rugs that she placed by both sides of the bed and a larger version of them in front of the fireplace were shades of the forest. As Don entered the room, Parker put plants in planters all around the space, some of them hanging from the window for the brightness of the sun.

"This is beautiful." She smiled at Don. "I love that you didn't want to add a television or any kind of computer table. This room is only for two things—sleeping and making love to you."

"To be honest, it never occurred to me to put either of those in here. I know we more than likely will have a television at some point, but again, it wasn't a top thing on my list of household things I'd like to have." Don made his way toward her, and she smiled at him as she waited. "I beat you here, so I get to be first."

"First to come? I don't have a problem with that. The first to be naked? Again, I have no trouble with that either. What would you like to be first at, Parker?" Parker wanted to be first in all things. Touching him. Having him touch her. Her mind was working overtime trying to come up with one thing she'd like to do at this moment. "You're thinking much too hard for someone who is about to rock my world."

"How do you know I will? I mean, I could be really terrible at this." He touched his fingers to her forehead and then down her cheek. "I could easily come just with your touch, Don. You have no idea how long I've waited for you. Since I was a child, I wanted someone to save me."

"I'll love you forever, Parker. Saving you is a pleasure. But I want you to know, you're going to save me, from a lifetime of being alone. You'll keep the sadness at bay. The happiness that I've discovered already will forever be mine." Parker said three words, words she never thought to utter to anyone, when she told him she loved him. "And I love you. With all my being. I will cherish you, keep you safe, and love you for all time."

Don took her blouse off her. The buttons seemed to just pull open under his touch. The warmth of his lion was keeping her from being cold or nervous while he touched her. And he did. Don touched her skin, every inch of it he exposed. Not just with his fingers, but his mouth and tongue.

Her skin was on fire for him, her body wet with need. As he dropped to his knees in front of her, Parker held her breath as he stripped her out of her shorts and panties. Holding onto the footboard of their bed, she watched as he licked her flowing cream from her knee to her pussy. She nearly came when he touched her with his tongue. Before she could tell him she'd already had enough, he took her clit into his mouth and suckled at her hard.

Parker came three times before she was able to catch her breath. If anyone had done that to her before, made her come so hard, she might well have become addicted to sex. She'd never been happier than she was right now with Don giving her such pleasure.

"You have anything in mind you'd like to be first at?" It took her befuddled mind a good deal longer than she thought it should have to understand the words coming out of his mouth. Nodding, then shaking her head, she told him she was too satisfied to think right now. "Well, I guess I'll have to do the thinking for the two of us."

When he picked her up into his arms, she felt light, cherished even. As soon as he dropped her to the bed and she bounced a couple of times before she settled, all thought of romance went out the window. Then he took off his shirt.

The fur of his lion was evident on his chest. She'd never cared for hairy men, but Don made it look too good for her to resist. Touching his nipples, making them harden for her, she sat on the edge of the bed and suckled hard on the tips. His fingers in her hair drove her to be more adventurous. Taking a small nip of his flesh there had him pushing her back on the bed and him following her.

He was naked, gloriously so. His muscles were tight, his flesh warm. Everywhere she touched him, she wanted to explore more of him. There didn't seem to be an end of places she could touch and massage.

"You're beautiful." She couldn't speak then. Her mouth was dry, her body so tensed up she felt as if she could have been shoved through the eye of a needle and come out unscathed. "I love you, Parker. Will you marry me?"

"Yes. Forever." Her fingers danced over his groin, then she wrapped her hand around his cock. It was too large for her hand; her fingers didn't touch. "Take me, Don. I want to feel you inside of me. I need to feel you make me yours."

He wouldn't be rushed. Don took his time with her, making her beg for him to give her relief one second, then telling him she'd had enough the very next one. Her body was putty for him. Parker had come so many times she was sure he was going to kill her before they'd even started their life together. When he leaned over her, his body stiff over hers, she watched his eyes as he filled her, his cock making her a part of his body so they could be one.

Parker saw him then, the lion that he was. The beast rolled over his skin, so she felt his fur under her roaming hands. His mane emerged where his beard would have been. The feel of it touching her breast, even for that second of touch, made her come hard.

Don took her harder then. His body over hers felt like a lifeline to her. Holding onto him, wrapping her legs around his hips, she threw back her head when she came again and screamed until she was hoarse with it.

He didn't join her as she went limp in his arms. Don ordered her to come again, then again, until she was virtually spent with it. But as soon as he threw back his own head, she felt a pause in the magic around them. The room grew to a deadly silence. Then he filled her.

Nothing could have prepared her for the connection. It snapped into her mind like a rubber band hitting her skin. As he roared, a beautiful lion's roar, she came again, seeing stars behind her eyelids, rainbows around his head. Holding onto her, Don dropped over her.

Both of them were breathing harshly. Her body didn't just go limp, but she was sure she'd lost a few parts of herself somewhere in the big bed. Rolling to his back, he let her lie beside him. She wasn't sure she could have stood him touching her right now. Her body was on hyperdrive or something. She was sure she'd been electrocuted.

Closing her eyes, she laid there with Don. Sleep would have been easy to fall into, but something around her moved. Not anything physical, but mentally, Parker felt something move toward her. Getting out of bed when she heard Don snore a little, she dressed herself as she left the bedroom.

Reaching beyond where she was, Parker realized she could stretch her magic further than ever before. When she touched on the disturbance, she knew it had to be her mother. But, and this frightened her a little bit, her mother was terrified of something. Or someone. Parker couldn't tell because whatever she was into, it was impossible to touch anything on her mind for more than a second. Things were moving around too fast for her to feel what was making her so upset. When there was a pause, unlike anything she'd ever felt in someone's head before, Parker waited, not even moving to figure out what was going on now.

Hello, daughter.

Parker screamed when the voice spoke to her, loud enough to pull Don's lion and have him rushing to her. She felt the earth move under her, the trees outside the house shimmer and shake hard enough that branches fell. Stones lifted out of their centuries old resting place. Even water, great falls, paused in flowing over their peak mountains with the magic she released in the scream.

What happened? She looked at Don, his lion as close to her as her own breath was. *What's happened? What do you need for me to do for you? Honey, you're scaring us both.*

"My father. He spoke to me." He didn't comment. What the hell could he say, really? "My father, I think, is within my mother."

Chapter 4

Meggie didn't move from the bench when someone sat beside her. Looking around wasn't an option either. Sitting very still was the only way she could assure herself of getting some quiet time. Park was silent right now, and she didn't want anything to wake him. Even if she had to sit there in the boiling sun, she'd do it.

He was going to kill her. There wasn't anything she could do about it either. But when she got a few minutes without him screaming at her to do things, things she'd never done before, Meggie would enjoy it for as long as she could.

Before long, he'd take over her body. He'd already taken over most of her day to day life. She could barely sleep, and eating was impossible unless he was sleeping or whatever he did when he wasn't yelling at her. As soon as he woke, it was go-go-go until she literally dropped.

"Mrs. Carter?"

She glanced at the man. Meggie didn't know him. Using the obvious sign one used to shut someone up, she put her finger to her lips and shushed him. When he entered her head, giving her a little nudge to tell her he was there, sort of like knocking on her door, she turned to look at him and, using sign language, told him once again to be quiet.

When he signed back at her, he told her he was the mate to her daughter. Meggie nearly screamed at him to tell her to stay away. She needed to keep away from her for as long as she could. Forever sounded good.

"She feels your pain now. And your husband spoke to her." Meggie asked him when this had happened and what he'd said. After he told her, she looked around to see if her daughter was nearby. "Parker isn't close. She can see you, but she's not going to show herself to you."

"Good. As much as I'd like to see her, there is no telling what he'll do to me to get at her. So if he wakes, I shall have to ignore you both. This man is killing me." He said he could see that she was ill. "Not ill. He's draining me. He wants me to find my Pa—your mate. Don't say her name. It wakes him from whatever he's doing in my body when he gives me peace. The man I married was never a good person. But now that he's gone forever, or so I thought, he's ten times the monster he was. He wants her to come to him willingly so that he can take her body as his own."

"Her magic as well, I'm betting." She smiled at the

young man. So he was smart. He might just be able to save her. "How did he get to be with you? I mean, even the few people I've spoken to about this are unsure how it happened. There is nothing in the books that we've looked at either. We wish to help you if you want him gone."

She didn't know either. What had happened the day he was killed was all she knew, and even that really didn't explain much. Like not only how he got to be a part of her, but how he had been killed.

"I was home resting. My husband was in the yard, testing my child on what she could do. Any fool could see she was stronger than him, but he insisted on training her. But it got out of hand that day. More than that day, I've come to realize. He was strangling her when he was killed." Don told her he'd heard that from her daughter. "She always let him train her like she was going to learn something new from him. But all it did was frustrate her when she wanted to just be normal. Which, I'm sure you've noticed, she wouldn't have been. I'm betting now she's more powerful than she was that day."

"I know who killed him. And the why of it. But even he hasn't any idea how your husband is here now with you." Meggie told him there were books in her home he could have if he wished. They had been her husband's. "I would love to have them. I'll send someone to get them when I leave here. Thank you for that."

"You'll have to send your wife, I'm afraid. She'll

know where to find them." He nodded. "Tell her they're in the lockbox. That's where I hid them."

"His head was removed. I'm thinking at some point prior to when he was killed, he gave all he was to you. I have no idea why he'd do something like that. As far as I know, he's not going to be able to survive in his current situation for much longer." Meggie told him she wasn't going to either. "I'm sorry about that as well. We're looking to see what we can find to save you. Most people say you're insane. I'm sorry. I think we both thought that as well."

"I'm not. I never liked him, not in all the years we were together. When I was pregnant with my daughter, he made me practice every day on things that were well over what I should have ever been able to do. He thinks that's why she's so good at magic, that he trained her." Don asked if that was the reason her husband thought he should have her magic. "Yes. He feels she slighted him in some way, and he wants her to give herself over to him. Freely."

When he looked up, Meggie turned in the direction he was looking as well. Not having any idea who the young woman across the street from them was, Meggie turned back to the man. The look on his face, the face of someone in love, said he was willing to sacrifice all he was for this other person. Turning back, Meggie realized it was her daughter.

"Good lord, she's beautiful." Don nodded and said

she was. "She looks so much like her grandfather. It hurts me."

"Is he still around? I mean, magic is in your bloodline, correct? Perhaps he knows of something we can use to separate the two of you. If he knew how you were suffering with his son inside of you, then he'd willingly help. Don't you think?" Meggie realized something in that moment. He didn't know. Neither of them knew. "Can I get his name so we can see what he might know?"

"The man inside of me, he isn't my daughter's biological father. I thought she knew that." Don must have spoken to her daughter because she watched her shake her head. "I was going to have a child before we were wed. I think it was the only reason he married me. He thought, because of my bloodline, I was going to be giving him more than he already had in the way of magic. Instead, he gave me more than I had. I wasn't magical at all before that. Oh, I could light a candle. Bring a book to me. Small things. Park could do extraordinarily little more than I could at the time. But the man who is her father, he's—he was magical. Very much so. As for her grandfather? I'm not sure. I saw him a few times when I was still living at home, but after I married this man, I was sort of cut off from everything."

"What happened to her father? You said was—is he dead?" Meggie told him what had happened. "So this man inside you, he's not above killing anyone for what he wants? He killed your mate so he could marry you.

Did he know about your daughter? Or I guess the other man's daughter?"

"No. Neither of them did. I knew, of course, but I never got around to telling Peter. Peter Windchaser, the Third." She felt the stirring of Park and looked at her daughter again while speaking to Don. "He's awake. Go. Save her from us. Please?"

The man didn't move as Park began screaming at her for not waking him like she was supposed to shake him awake when all she wanted to do was rest — or get rid of him. Glancing at the man, she watched as he signed to her again. This time, she could only nod at what he was asking her.

"I can find him with the name you gave me. Whoever he is or how strong he is, he might explain how this man is inside of you, killing you. Also, why Parker is so strong. She is, you know. Stronger than any witch she knows."

Meggie looked away when he asked her if she needed anything. All she wanted was to be alone from now on. Meggie thought the only way she was going to be able to be alone, for things to be back to normal, was to kill herself. The idea of it had been on her mind for the last several days since she'd left her hometown to come here. Park was going to hurt her more and more daily until she was just too weak to fight him anymore. She knew it as surely as she knew he was going to hurt Parker.

"What the fuck are you doing?" She didn't answer him. It was better if she didn't try and explain herself to him. "Do you know where she is? Have you done a damned thing I've asked you to do? I doubt it. All you've done is whine whine whine. Well, when Parker turns her magic over to me, I'm going to murder you first thing. I'm sick of you, and your not liking the way things are going. Get up and find her."

Meggie was so sore. Her body ached in several places, worse than when she'd given birth to Parker. Her feet were blistered because she was forever walking to one place or another. Not to mention, her intake of both food and water were way down. It was her way, she supposed, to get back at Park for what he was doing to her. The less she took care of herself, the weaker he became. It was all she knew how to do to save her child.

Avoiding the building where her daughter had been, she walked around the little square in the town. The entire trip was spoiled for her, as Park never shut up about what she wasn't doing for him. As she was making the second turn in the little park, Meggie nearly ran, but she wasn't sure which way to go. Her daughter stood in front of her. Then she did something that Meggie hadn't had done to her in years—she hugged her.

"Father, come forth." Meggie cried out in pain. Only for a second, however. Parker touched her, and just like that, the pain disappeared. She also noticed that Park was suddenly silent again as if he were hiding behind her. "Park Carter, I, Parker Megan Carter, high witch, demand that you come forth and speak to me."

She could feel Park's pain then. His screams as he struggled to ignore Parker told her he was losing the battle. When he screamed again, she felt him pull from her body, just enough that she could see him as he did what Parker demanded of him.

It was surreal for her to see this thing coming from her body. It was Park, she could see that. However, it wasn't. Meggie could see where his head had been reattached to his shoulders. The blood was thick and sticky, like a necklace of it. When he growled, at who Meggie didn't know, she felt somewhat better than she had since he'd been killed all those years ago.

"You will leave this body you've taken for your own." Park told Parker he wasn't going anywhere. "You will. Willingly or not, you will leave her, and you will move on to wherever you were to go when your life was taken from you."

"You are mine. I have always known you'd be the one that would make me important to the magical world." Arms wrapped around Meggie from behind. It was Don, feeding her energy to keep her upright and stronger. "You would have been nothing without me there for you all the time. I will say when I will leave. You will, Parker, give yourself over to me so I can become the greatest warlock ever created."

"Not going to happen, moron." Parker lifted her hands into the sky. It was a sight Meggie knew she'd never forget. Magic, strong white magic surrounded

Parker like a blanket. When she shoved it forward, she knew that Park was going to be hurt. And badly. "Sleep."

If not for Don holding her, Meggie was sure she would have been falling backward. As soon as Don stepped away, leaving her to stand on her own, Meggie waited for Park to retaliate. When there was nothing from him, not even his painful reminder that he was inside of her, Meggie looked at her daughter.

"He won't bother you for a couple of days. It might be longer. I don't know how strong he is now, but at least we can plot his demise and get his ass out of you." Meggie couldn't help it. Bursting into tears, she wrapped her arms around Parker and was ever so happy when she hugged her back. "Mom, I had no idea. I didn't know anything until he spoke to me last night. I would have come to you first thing."

Meggie was babbling as she told Parker what he'd been doing to her. His plans for Parker. The words just spilled out of her like a fountain, but she was glad Parker didn't tell her to shut up and start over. Pulling back, she looked at her daughter. Really looked at her.

"I never thought to see you again. I didn't think you'd want anything to do with me after Park tried to kill you." Parker told her it was done and to move on. "I can't. I have this monster inside of me. For now, he's quiet, but he won't be forever. You have to kill me, Parker. Kill me so the world will be rid of the monster he's become."

"I'm not going to kill you, Mom. I might have to hurt

you a little to get him free of you, but I won't kill you. But I'm going to see my grandda in a couple of days. I'll also pick up the books. I want you to stay with us." Meggie told her she couldn't do that. What if Park woke again? "I'll deal with him again. He has to know by now that he's bitten off more than he could ever hope to chew. He's going to regret everything he's done to both of us."

Meggie thought Parker was right. Park would regret tangling with her little girl. As she got into the big car that pulled up beside them, Meggie thought of all the things she could now tell her daughter. Everything she knew, too, about how to find the books she'd hidden from Park. Hopefully, Parker could make some sense of the ramblings of Park. She certainly couldn't.

~~~

Don was in love. Smiling to himself, he thought of how stupid that sounded. Of course, he loved his mate. But it was like when he saw her in different circumstances he'd fall in love with her again. She was, he thought, the most brilliant person he'd ever met.

When his cell phone rang, he went out on the back deck to answer it. Jasper was at their home with Meggie and Parker right now, and it was difficult for him to hear his own thoughts, much less that of the person calling him. Don was surprised to see the call was from the principle of the school where he taught.

"Mr. Foster, I would like to speak to you. As soon as possible, if you have a few minutes." Don told him he had a few minutes right now if he wanted to talk. "Good. I'd like for you to take over the football team for the high school. I know you already have a full load, what with teaching math and science to the students, but you could easily turn one of those over to another teacher when we hire someone."

Don didn't know what to say. First of all, he thought the school had a good football coach, even though they'd not won a game in longer than he could remember right now. Also, he loved math and science and would hate to give up either one of the classes. As he was thinking, Mr. Martin began speaking again.

"The new teachers we've hired won't be as good as you have been at teaching. But the kids really like you, and I think that is most of why you're such a good teacher." That didn't sound like he was complimenting him, so he waited again. "The sign-ups for football have started, and you'll have to get with the other coaches as soon as possible to weed out the kids that won't make us look good. Then there —"

"Hang on a second. I didn't say I'd take the job." Mr. Martin assured him it would be easy for him to do. "Perhaps it might be, but I have to think on it. I've recently married, and I don't want to be spending most of my time away from home right now."

"Well, I'm sorry to hear that. I've already told the other coaches you're going to be in charge." Don wasn't sure if Martin was sorry he'd taken a wife or that he wasn't willing to just take the job. He asked him why he'd tell the other coaches that without talking to him. "I just assumed you'd do it, I guess. You will. I don't know why you think playing hardball about it is going to make any difference. You're perfect for the job. And if you could, talk your sister-in-law into paying for the new uniforms I've ordered. Your family helping me out will go a long way in making sure the kids have something to wear on the field that isn't twenty years old."

"It sounds to me like you only want me to take this job because I have a wealthy sister-in-law." Mr. Martin said that helped. "I'm not going to talk to her about forking over money for the football team. Whether I decide to take the job or not."

"I'm sorry to hear that. I told you we're hiring new teachers, didn't I? Well, it wouldn't be any more effort for me to hire someone to take your job from you as well. I told you, I've ordered the uniforms and made it clear you're to be in charge. I'm going to have to ask you to step down as teacher if you don't help out the school district on this." Don asked him if he was blackmailing him. "No. I'd not call it that. Blackmail sounds like such a horrendous thing. I'm only saying if you can't do this thing, taking the team to state with nice new uniforms, you're not someone I can trust to do a good job in teaching. I'm sure you can understand that."

"I think I do." Parker joined him on the deck, and he looked at her as he asked Mr. Martin when he needed his answer. "I have to talk to my wife about this. Not to mention, I'm going to have to find a way to work this in with my already overloaded schedule."

"You need to let me know when you're going to go to the football field by tomorrow. They're all waiting on you today, but I can put them off one more day." Don thought they'd be waiting an exceedingly long time if he had anything to do with it. "You just show up in the morning at eight and get them going in the right direction. I'll set up a little to-do to thank your sister-in-law for helping us out. You too, but that doesn't have to be common knowledge. I'll be seeing you, Don. And thanks for doing this for us."

He didn't bother pointing out again that he'd not said he'd take the job but closed the connection. Don looked at Parker when she smiled at him. He told her what had been said and what he thought of taking the job.

"I've been trying to be the assistant football coach since I started teaching there. But there was always someone with more experience than me. I never gave it much credence before. We'd win or lose. It was just fun for me to be able to go to the games on Friday night with my brothers when they were home." Parker asked him what he wanted to do. "I don't know, to be honest. I feel as if I'm going to lose out either way I go. But I'm not going to tell Brook about this."

"I would." Don asked her why. "Because he involved her when he blackmailed you into taking the job. Or not taking it, I guess you could say. I'd tell her simply because the decision for her to donate or not is up to her. Not you and your job."

"I suppose." He loved teaching, but not at the risk of pissing off Brook. "I'll talk to her now. She might have a different opinion than I do about how this went down. I think, as you said, it's straight-up blackmailing, but I might just be reading too much into it."

"No, you're not, and you know it." He did. Don thought that was what had hurt him so much about this. He would have willingly taught both classes and worked with the football team. But now it seemed dirty somehow. "Let your sister know. Brook will not only take care of the jerk, but you might also be the coach when that dumbass is fired."

He decided she was right. Pulling out his phone again, he put it on speaker so Parker could hear Brook's end of the conversation. As soon as Don told her everything that was going on, she started cursing. Don was hard-pressed not to join Parker in laughing at her.

"You mean that son of a bitch blackmailed you? I'm telling you right now, Don, if he even— Christ, I want to go there and beat the shit out of him." Don laughed. "This isn't funny. I swear to you, I'm going to make sure everyone understands what he's done today."

"But it will be his word against mine. And we both know I don't have nearly the amount of support he does." Brook asked him why he'd think that. "I'm nothing but a teacher, while he's been my boss for all these years. He could, and it's happened before, say he's been covering for me for all my career—something along the lines of child pornography material on my computer. Or I've been caught with some of the team, and that's why I'm not good enough to be their coach. He could and will ruin me."

"I would never let that happen." He told Brook she might not be able to stop it. "I'm going to work on this. I have to take care that he doesn't get away with something like this again. Or, for that matter, if he has been doing this all along, and you're the first person to come forward with it."

"I don't know. But you might want to start with the girls' softball team. It only just occurred to me that they didn't have a coach until a week before school started last year. They also got new uniforms." Brook asked him if he knew her name. "Yes. Mildred Angler. She's from town, I believe. I don't see her much. She's also carrying a huge load of classes she teaches, as well as going to college herself. The last time I did get to speak to her, she wondered how she was going to be a good doctor if she couldn't handle a few hard days. It would be a shame to lose her to teaching when she might be the next person to cure something like cancer. Don't you think?" Brook said she'd get back to him.

After putting his phone away, he asked Parker how things were going. When she sat down and put her feet up on his lap, he pulled her sandals off and massaged her ankles. She moaned, and he did as well.

"I'm betting that if I were to moan three or four times a minute, you'd be stone-hard all the time." He told her it wouldn't even take that much. "Why? Are you telling me you're hard all the time or something different?"

"I'm hard from the time I wake in the morning until I sleep at night. Hell, for all I know, I'm hard while I'm sleeping." When she laughed, Don smiled at her. "You want to tell me what it is you're avoiding telling me? I have a feeling it's not good, whatever it is."

"I don't want my mom to die. I've missed a great deal by being apart from her, and I'm not ready for her to leave me because of Park." Don asked her what she was going to do. "I don't know for certain right now. She wants me to kill her, so it will kill him. Jasper has gone to get the books she hid away from Park, as well as the ones he'd been using. Also, I've contacted my biological grandfather, and he wants nothing to do with me. He claims, and there isn't any reason for him not to believe that I've sullied his name and that of his family by being arrested for murder. No amount of talking to him will change his mind."

"I will." She told him he didn't have to do that. "Oh, but I do. I have to be your knight in shining armor on something. You're my life, and I want to do this for you."

"You just think you're going to get laid if you talk him into it." Don smiled at her. "You're not as cute and sexy as you think you are. Just putting that out there."

"Perhaps not, but I can make you scream better than anything on this earth. And you do that so well too." Sticking her tongue out at him only had him moaning again. "You keep that up, and your mom is going to have a first-hand view of what I do to you to make you come. She's coming out here now."

Parker looked up at her mom when she came out onto the deck with them. He didn't stop massaging her feet and laughed when Meggie told him she'd give anything for someone to have done that for her. Offering his services had her turning him down, which was what he expected. Parker asked her if she needed anything.

"Yes. I was wondering if you have a car I can borrow, or even that limo for a few hours. I want to get some things cleared away while Park is not bothering me. I need to sell my house, and I have some things at the house I'd like for you to have. They were your father's." Parker said she could take her. "I think I'd like that. I would. Do you mind if I borrow Parker for a few hours?"

"Not at all. I have some things I have to take care of as well today." He stood up when Parker put her feet down on the deck. "As you can see, I've been dismissed from being helpful here."

They were both still giggling as they entered the house. Don turned and looked behind him when he heard a familiar sound. He knew it was one of his brothers standing just in the tree line, but from here, he couldn't tell which one of them it was. Moving to the side of the house where he couldn't be seen by Meggie, he let his lion take him.

Running in the direction his brother Quin had gone, he was glad for the distraction. He'd not been on a good run since meeting Parker. As soon as he spotted his brother, the two of them ran full out as they dodged fallen and standing trees. It was better than he thought it would be, getting his head cleared out before he had to tackle Mr. Windchaser. Then, no doubt, the school board when the shit hit the fan with Mr. Martin. He told Quin about the two things he had on his plate when they sat down by the river and rested.

You're not going to allow them to run you off, are you? He said he didn't know what he was going to do. The ball was sort of in Brook's park. *Yeah, well, that's scarier than anything I could have thought of to get someone to straighten up. Can you imagine what she'll be like when their kids are born? I'd hate to be one of her kids' teachers. You might want to think about retiring before then. She'll kick your ass even if her kid is the one at fault.*

I think her kids would be wonderfully calming for her. Quin snorted. *They might be. Or, and this is more along the lines of what you were saying, they might be holy terrors that come to school armed and dangerous. I think you're right. I'm going to retire before I have to teach any of her children.*

The two of them sat there for a couple of hours, bantering back and forth on what sort of children each of them would have. By far, they both thought that they'd not want to deal with Brook or her kids. Even Ronan would be hard to deal with if they were hooligans.

He might be one of the nicest guys you'd ever want to meet. But mess with his kids, then he'd be the king lion that he is. Quin agreed with him. *Christ, I just had a thought. What will happen when I'm a father?*

Every time Quin glanced in his direction, he would start laughing. Don wished he'd not voiced his concern in such a tone, nor as loudly as he had. It was a frightening thought for him to be a dad. Something else he thought of but kept to himself, what if his kid was more magical than either he or Parker? It bore thinking about.

Chapter 5

Peter had a daily routine. It wasn't a habit, as his wife used to tell him, but a routine. He would come down after he'd showered and dressed for the day and drink a cup of hot English tea while he read the newspaper. After that, he'd have a coddled egg with a single piece of buttered rye toast. He didn't want to be bothered by anyone or anything while he was doing his routine, either. But he did admit, only to himself, he certainly missed his wife fussing at him all the time.

"Mr. Windchaser?" He looked at his long time butler and hoped he would see the anger in his face and go away. "Sir, there is a phone call for you. The man said it's important that he speak to you now. It's a life or death emergency."

"I don't care what it's about. I don't like to have my morning start off in this manner, Jacob. Did you tell him that? That I hate being interrupted like this?" Jacob said he had, several times as a matter of fact. "Yet he's still going to do it. I'll tell you right now if this is a hoax to get me to donate to some cause, I'm going to own it by the end of the day, and then I'm going to close it down. See if I don't. Bring me the blasted phone."

Shoving his cup of tea and paper out of the way, he knew he'd not be in the mood to read it or to enjoy his tea. Damned people. Didn't they listen anymore? It was more than likely some person wanting him to endorse them on some hairbrained idea.

When the phone was handed to him, Peter barked into the thing, telling the person to get on with what they had to say to him.

"I know who killed your son. Also, the reason behind it." Whatever he thought the person might have said to him, that certainly hadn't ever entered his mind. "My name is Donahue Foster. Everyone just calls me Don. I'm a local teacher. The man who killed your son is Park Carter. You might know him as well."

"Who is this?" The man repeated his name without sounding the least bit sorry for making him upset. "Why are you calling me now? My son has been gone for several years now. I don't think they have ever caught the man who killed him. Yet here you are, after all the police and agents I had working on it, telling me not only that you know who it was, but you know his name as well. Why would you do that? Bring this up now. After all these years."

"I'm married to your granddaughter. Her name is Parker Foster." He said he wasn't related to that person. "Are you sure, Mr. Windchaser? To look at her, I'd say she's the spitting image of you and your late wife. I'm sorry for your loss, but Parker could have been her twin when she was younger. She also has your wife's eye color. She's beautiful."

"I'm guessing you want me to claim this so-called twin of mine so you can get all my money when I pass on. Are you going to kill me too? I wouldn't put it past anyone that would call at this time of the morning." The man started to speak again, but Peter cut him off. "No. I won't put up with this. This is the same thing that killed my poor wife, Peggy. It cut her to the quick to know someone out there had killed our only child and then got away with it. Do you think you're the first person to have tried this? You're not. More than likely, you won't be the last in my lifetime, either."

"Parker is magical. An extraordinarily strong witch who has powers that haven't been seen in decades. She can not only see the future, Mr. Windchaser, but she can also give a person immortality. Your son could do that. Couldn't he?" Peter didn't dignify his question with an answer. "His wife to be, Meggie Steward, was a victim as much as you and your wife were. She not only witnessed her only love's death but bore him a child that inherited all his magic."

"Listen here, Mr. Foster. You're going to have

to do better than that to get me to believe this child is my granddaughter. As I said, I've had this done to us before." He thought of his delicate wife and how it had destroyed her when one after the other crackpots came to say they had information on their son. "You come up with a better plan about this, and I might grant you a few minutes of my time. As it is right now, I've—"

"Parker has a mark on her back, on the left side just below the ribs. It's a mark of magic. Also, a mark that your family has handed down to generation after generation of Windchaser magical holding members." Before he could stop himself from speaking the words flowing in his mind, his mouth asked the younger man what it looked like. "It's a broom. There is a cat beneath it that is as white as snow. I'm to understand that if a member of the family is born with a black cat or any other dark color of a cat, they're shunned from the family and aren't heard of again."

"I don't believe you." Don told him it mattered little to him if he did or didn't, but the facts were clear. "What is it you want from me? Money? I'm not so easily separated from my money or anything else I own."

"I don't need or want your money, Mr. Windchaser. If you were near a computer, I could send you a picture of the mark if you'd like." Peter asked him what price he put on him knowing this. "You mean you think I'm going to charge you for a chance to get to know the only other living person that is related to you? No, I'm not.

Money isn't a problem for either me or Parker. I'd like to think I'm a better man than that. I'd do this for you even if I didn't have two cents to rub together. Family is important to me. I'm putting this on you so you can make your own decisions about whether or not you wish to be a family with Parker. Also, any children we will have."

"Come now. You can't expect me to believe you have all the money in the world at your fingertips, do you? Even I, as wealthy as I am, still look for a good deal. What makes you so special that you think you're above making a profit off maybe showing me my granddaughter?"

Peter was laughing when the man spoke. He wasn't quite sure he heard him right and asked him to repeat it.

"I said, my brother, is married to someone you know. Brook Garrett Foster. She asked me to remind you of the beautiful design she did for your offices not long ago. And how you made the front page of all the newspapers in the world for being such a forward thinking man. Also, she said your business tripled because of it. Brook said she never took credit for it or would ever do that to you. You're a good man, she told me." Peter stood up and made his way to his computer. Telling the man what his email address was, he was logging into the Internet when his watch told him he had an email. "Mr. Windchaser, I don't want you to think I don't need anything from you since we've gotten this far. But I have a magical issue that I believe you can help me with. It's how to rid someone of a specter that has taken over a living body. Without permission, I might add."

The picture was as clear as if the woman baring her back to the camera was right there in the room with him. Touching his fingers to the sigil on her, he thought of his son and the exact same mark on him. Peter wondered for a moment if the young man speaking to him had any idea what it meant to be marked like this. More than likely not, he thought, or he would have told him. The mark was his son's. Peter had no doubt about that now.

"You've my address, I'm assuming." Don told him he was near enough to see his home. "You might as well come in then. I think we have a great deal to speak about. Is she with you? Parker, I think you called her. Is she with you right now?"

"She can be. Right now, she's taking care of another issue with the school board that's blackmailing me." Peter laughed. It startled him, his own laughter. He'd not heard it in so long he'd forgotten what a terrible sound it made. But right now, he just didn't care. A granddaughter. She was out there, and he was going to get to meet her. "You come on in, Mr. Foster. I'm willing to see you. But I swear to you, if this is a joke, I'm going to be highly upset with you. And don't think I won't take action against you either. You tell that sister-in-law of yours that too."

Peter made his way to the door. Opening it before the man could touch the doorbell, he stood there staring at the man and woman standing there. If he lived to be a hundred years old, he'd still remember this day more than anything else in his life. It was as if his wife, the day he asked her to marry him, was standing in front of him again.

"You look like my Peggy." The woman smiled at him, and he could see she'd gotten her smile from him. "I miss her more and more every day. But if she were here right now, with the two of you, you can bet she'd be telling me I told you so. She said she felt a child of Peter's was alive and well someplace. You're my granddaughter, aren't you, honey?"

"I think so. You're nothing like I expected. I thought you'd be an old man with a rod up your ass and no compassion at all." Peter wasn't sure if she was joking or not, so just stared at her. "I am kidding. I just wanted to test your sense of humor."

"I have none. I used to, but people took that right out of me." She asked him if he was going to invite them in. "I don't know. Are you planning to be a smart ass the entire time you're here?"

"Yes, as a matter of fact. Are you going to be an old bastard while I'm trying to get you to laugh?" He told her more than likely. "Oh well. I guess we can't pick who we're related to. Can we? Hello, Grandda. I'm so awfully glad to meet you."

And just like that, he fell in love with her. Not only that, but Peter drew her to him and hugged her like she was his only lifeline in the world. Christ, his baby had a baby. And here she stood. As beautiful as anything he'd ever had the pleasure of looking at before.

"I'm sorry. I'm never this emotional." Parker said he was leaking too. "I most certainly am not leaking. Darn it, girl, have you no respect for your elders?"

"Not in the least bit. What you see is what you get with me." She made him laugh again, and he thought he was getting better at it. "You really aren't anything I thought you'd be. When we found that you lived in this big house, my first thought was that you'd turn me away for just the reasons you told Don. That you'd been fucked with before and had no intention of opening your heart up to anyone again. This is a stuffy house, you know."

"Yes, well, there hasn't been anyone living here but me and the staff for a long time. I'm probably handing you more to make fun of me about, but I think I was just waiting to die here. The staff would find my body in one of the rooms and just dump me in the back yard." Parker told him that's how she'd handle his corpse. "You do say what you want, don't you?"

"I do. There are a couple of things you should be made aware of. One, I was just released from prison. It took them eight years to figure out what I'd been saying all along. I didn't kill my stepfather. At the time, I thought he was my father, a cruel bastard that thought his shit didn't stink like everyone else's." He had read about her in the paper but hadn't really cared at the time. "Secondly, I'm not going to tolerate you treating my mother like shit. She's been through hell and back being married to Park. She didn't have a choice in marrying him. The marriage was something he maneuvered around so he could get her magic. Park thought since she was a witch from an extraordinarily strong family, he'd get more out of marrying her. It didn't work out that way for either of them."

"Meggie was engaged to Peter when he died. I don't think I treated her very well when she came to see my wife and me. We were still dealing with our own grief when she made her way to us. By the time I thought of her again, she was already married to that Park person. I just— Well, I just wrote her off, thinking she'd not really loved Peter at all." Parker told him she still mourned his passing. "As do I. Every day, I think of him, and it doesn't seem to hurt any less."

He invited them for a late breakfast. For the first time in all of his adult life, he changed up his routine. Not only did he enjoy having a scone with his breakfast, but also two cups of tea. Peter laughed too, more than he had in decades. There was something so rudely refreshing about Parker that made him want to tease her into some sort of debate.

He noticed, too, that Don loved Parker, and she did him. They were the most beautiful couple he'd ever seen together. Also, they seemed to enjoy life to the fullest. Don told him he was a lion. Peter had to admit, he'd never seen a lion, not even in a zoo setting.

"We're much larger than the ones in the zoo, sir.

My brother Ronan, he's the king of all lions all over the world. He and his wife Brook, they take their job very seriously." Peter asked him how much of a family he had. "I have five brothers and my mom and grandma. Grandma is living with my mom for now. And each of my brothers all have their own homes, thanks to Brook. I'm to understand you know her."

"I do. She's a pistol, that one." Don told him she'd gotten worse since marrying his brother. "That's hard to believe. I enjoy working with her. She's done several projects for me over the years. Never would have thought she'd have the guts to take on jobs like she has. She's made a name for herself; I will say that for her."

"We're all a little afraid of her. I think she likes that too." Peter laughed, catching himself off guard the way it just flowed from his mouth now. "I've been talking to my brother, Ronan. He would like you to come to his home for dinner tonight. Brook said to tell you it's at six, and you'll be there."

"I think I'd like that. Very much so." He looked at the couple and shook his head. "What I wouldn't give for my Peggy to be here to see you two. She'd have a fit about it. Now, tell me what it is you'd like to know about magic. I would like to explain, I have quite a bit myself, but not nearly as much as my son had or you have, Parker. But I have lots of notes and books that have been handed down from several generations of Windchaser's."

"May I take them to read over? I will return them to

you as soon as I'm finished." Peter, never one to make a decision on the cuff, did so in that moment. He told her they were hers to keep. As soon as he said the words, a weight, one he'd not known he had, lifted from not just his body, but from his soul as well. "Thank you for that. I have some that my mother's family had as well. If you'd like to read over those, you're more than welcome to them."

When Parker nodded, he had to look away. His wife, he thought—Peggy would have been over the moon right now. He was so happy that in his lifetime, he was not only able to get to know this girl but that he'd have plenty to tell Peggy about when he did meet up with her on the other side.

~~~

Quin rubbed the spot where he'd injected the little kitten. She wasn't going to make it. Giving her a shot to combat the pain he was sure she was in was about all he could do for her at this point. He was sure that the little girl who had found the kitten knew it as well. Anna asked him if she could sit with Ginger, the name she'd given the kitten, for a while.

"Yes. For as long as you wish. You did a good thing by bringing her in to me. I don't know if she has enough energy to save herself now, but she has a better chance than she did before." Anna nodded as she gently ran her fingers over her fur. "I'm sorry I can't do more for her, honey. She hasn't eaten for an exceptionally long time."

"I know you're doing all you can for her. I just don't understand people." He wisely kept his mouth shut. He didn't understand them either. "My mom said I could have a kitten when we moved here last month. But they're so expensive, you know?"

"Where are you looking? At the store? I'm sure once I put the word out that you're looking for a pet of your own, you'll have so many offers for one you'll have as many as your mom will allow you." She looked up at him, tears on her cheeks. "However, we don't want to rush things, now do we?"

"She's going to die, isn't she?" Quin got down to her level and nodded. "We did everything we could for her, too. I'm not sure how I can pay you, Doctor Quin, but I've got a birthday coming up, and I can give that money to you."

"I'm not going to charge you for this, Anna. You tried to save an animal, and in my books, that makes you a wonderful person. But don't think of this as just letting her die. She's not going to perish alone, and that is a good thing." Anna nodded as she petted the kitten.

Quin left her in the room. It was that, or he was going to join her in an all-out bawling event. It killed just a little of him every time he lost a patient. It was especially hard on him when a child was there to witness it. Going to the front, he smiled at his grandma as she played with the little bunny that had been brought in a couple of hours ago. She was talking to it while she played a game on his computer.

"I'll have you know I think working for you was a mistake. Your mother told me if I bring home one more animal, she's going to make me sleep in the shed and put all the creatures in my room. Do you think she's serious?" He told her she'd said the same thing to him when he was younger. "Well, she will have to get used to it all over again, I'm thinking. How's the little muffin in the room with the cat? It's not going to make it, is it?"

"She's taking it hard, but better than I am. I hate to lose a patient, you know." His grandma had been working for him for a few days now. While she seemed to enjoy it, he was worried she'd overdo on some of the heavier things that were needed to work in a vet's office. Like holding down a big animal while he tried to diagnose what was wrong with it. "Grandma, what would you think about me having a source for pets here for people to adopt?"

Quin laughed at himself. It wasn't even a thought until just then. Grandma winked at him and told him she would love it. The more they spoke about the idea of it, the more he liked it as well. Not just cats and dogs, though they were the most popular. Quin thought it would be fun to see if he could match up snakes and the like for people too.

Anna came out of the room a few minutes later. Grandma and he were still working on the other idea when Anna hugged him tightly from behind, telling him that Ginger was gone. He picked Anna up and held her as he wanted, tightly in his arms, to give comfort to her.

"I watched her breathing for a long time, and I saw that it was getting harder for her to do. Then she looked at me, and I knew she was thanking me for being there with her." Quin told her he was sure she was. "I held her little paw in my fingers until she closed her eyes and passed away. I'll never forget this, Doctor Quin. Not for as long as I live, will I forget how she died here with me by her side."

Putting Anna back down, he watched her as she stood telling his grandma how she'd come to find the little kitten in an abandoned building by her house. The rest of the litter, as well as the mother, were all dead. Anna didn't say it, but he had a feeling all of them had suffered badly. He'd asked Cass to go by and take care that they were buried properly.

"You need a job." He looked at his grandma when she spoke to Anna. "Yes, that's the ticket. You need a job. I'm much too busy working on the phones to have time to cuddle some of the animals brought in here by people. Look at this bunny. What am I to do while it's needing someone to make sure he knows he's loved?"

Grandma handed the bunny to Anna, and she asked what she was to do with it. She knew nothing about bunnies. His wonderful grandma said she didn't either but then asked Anna if she knew how to cuddle.

"I do. I mean, I think I do." The bunny snuggled up under Anna's chin when she sat in the other chair behind the desk Grandma was working at. "Why is he here? I mean, did someone drop him off and not stay to make sure he was going to be all right? That's not right. People can't just abandon animals like they're nothing."

"He was dropped off this morning when someone hit him. They have an allergy for bunnies, but they made sure he was going to be all right. Once I said that Mr. Whiskers here was stunned but not hurt, the man had to leave." She asked about the name. "That's what he'd been calling the bunny before he dropped it off. I think he was deeply sorry he couldn't take him home with him."

"What will happen to him now that he's all right? He's very friendly, isn't he?" Quin told her he'd contacted the people that owned him, and they were coming to get him later. "So you want me to just keep him company? I can do that. I would have to talk to my momma about working here. I don't think she'd care all that much."

"You talk to her if you want, honey. Even if there aren't any pets to cuddle with, you can come here and keep me company." Grandma looked at him. "Don't you have things to do? Go on now. I got this part handled."

"Yes, ma'am."

He kissed his grandma on the cheek. Her perfume, the scent of her lion, brought so many memories to his mind that he staggered just a little. Kissing her again, he thought about his grandma being around forever and did a little dance. He wanted his children to remember her scent too. Like gardenias and roses on a spring morning.

Going into the little room he had put the kitten in, Quin put her into a box made especially for the burial of small animals and wrote her name and day of her death on the top of it. Tomorrow he'd take her to the woods behind his mom's old place and bury her, a place he'd been burying animals since he'd been a little boy. Ronan contacted him just as he was putting Ginger in the freezer for tomorrow.

The people came out today to look at the old barn on Mom's land. He's going to work on it with Brook to see how much they can preserve and how much is going to have to be taken down. It looks to him like it might not have to be torn down at all. But if we end up doing that, you know how it is. In old places, you never know what you might find when you start working on it. Anyway, he wants to help Brook save as much of the original wood as they can. Get this — it'll be done in about a month if nothing goes wrong. He asked what they were planning to do with it. *Brook wants to insulate it so it can be used all the time. Mom wants it to have a full kitchen to use when someone wants to have a family gathering.*

That sounds good. If it's heated or air-conditioned, it might be the perfect place for weddings too. No matter the time of year. Ronan told him that was what Mom had told him. *I hired someone today. Well, Grandma did. Do you know the Harper family? I think it's just a little girl, Anna, and her mom. She's never mentioned a father. The girl brought in a kitten that was nearly gone. Can you look into them for me? The girl wants a kitten, but they're too expensive, she said. I thought she meant purchasing them, but now that I think on it, I think it might be the long term of having a cat and the bills associated with having one.*

I'll see what I can find out and get back to you. Hang on. Mom just walked in, and I'll speak to her. You know she would know if anyone else didn't.

He didn't wait on his brother to come back to him too soon. Picking up his office phone, he made some calls to the local shelter, asking how he could perhaps help them out by having pictures of pets available to be adopted posted on the office walls. They were so excited to let him help, someone was coming out with not just pictures but a kitten or two for Anna. He was also going to make sure the kid had enough money for food and other items.

Okay. They just moved here. He told Ronan he'd forgotten to mention that part. *No matter. Mom still knows who they are. The little girl is Anna, as you said. She's almost ten. The mom – her name is Shirley – is hiding out here from an abusive ex-husband. Shirley is having a hard time finding employment because she's not lived here long enough. Also, the ex-husband is an abusive prick, and the places where Shirley has applied are worried he might show up and cause some damage to not just the wife and daughter, but also to wherever she's working. Brook is going to hire her to work in the offices with her.*

Thanks. Ronan told him it was his pleasure. But he had to find her a place to live, so they'd be safe. *I can do that. I have two places in mind. One of them is close to where*

Brook's offices are.

By the time Quin was ready to call it a day, Shirley had met with Brook and had been hired. His brothers were helping her move the things she'd left home with into the house he'd found for them. And Anna had two kittens instead of one because the barn on the back of the property would need to have the mice cleared out. He knew that any house his family was in or lived near wouldn't have any trouble with rodents of any kind, but he wanted Anna to have something of her own. The kittens were the perfect balm for her broken heart since the last kitten had died. And the shelter was so excited to have an outlet to advertise their animals, they gave her a month of food as well as some toys for her and the kittens to play with. A good start all the way around, he thought.

As he was walking home that night, he thought about what might be in store for him if his mate were to come around. He'd be in trouble, he knew it. Quin wasn't easy to get along with most of the time. Having a mate around all the time would cause him to have to seek out his own time. He only hoped she was an animal lover. Otherwise, he was going to hate giving up his job for her. Quin would, but he'd not be happy about it.

Smiling at himself, Quin thought he had a long time to get used to the idea of having a mate. Something far off, he was thinking. Or hoping. He wasn't quite sure which. Going into the house, he looked around. He supposed he'd better start getting some things to put in the house besides a card table that was older than him and a lawn chair to sit at it.

Or maybe not. He hadn't any idea why, but he thought of his house as a clean slate. Whoever came to be his mate, she'd have this, all of it, to work with. Laughing at himself, he knew he was about as bad at decorating as he was at socializing. Quin really sucked at both.

Chapter 6

Clyde Martin was enjoying his time watching the football team get ready for the new season. To him, it was the best kind of sport to have at a high school level. There was little to no involvement on his part. The kids that played had to pay the school for their equipment. The concession stands made so much money because parents donated some of the products they sold. And since he'd made a deal with the coaches around the area, he was going to be making money off of holding the football camp here—a win-win for the school, but mostly him.

Now that he'd gotten the right people in place to train them, they could fill up the new trophy cabinet quicker. It was also his plan to have more seating. The more butts that came to a game was more money all the way around for him and his little projects.

Having Don Foster as their coach, the all-American Player winner two years in a row when he'd been going here, was just the ticket he needed for the papers to recognize him as being the best principal in the state. He'd like to be known as the best in the country, but he didn't want to seem too greedy this soon.

Glancing at his watch, he saw that Don had twenty minutes to get here and get started. He'd heard from Brook just yesterday—she wanted a meeting to discuss the uniforms. Things were falling into place better than he'd thought. Soon the money from the players' parents to help pay for the new uniforms would be sitting nicely in his own account. He was going to make sure no one knew Brook Foster had paid for them in full. Yes, he liked it when all his ducks lined up in a nice neat row.

"Mr. Martin?" He smiled at the young player and asked him why he wasn't on the practice field. "I have a note here for you. Mr. Ronan said I was to give it to you. Also, my mom said I can't play football."

Before he could ask him why she'd say such a thing, three more kids came to stand by him, telling him the same thing. Their parents said they couldn't play football. This time, however, he got to ask one of the kids what the reasoning was behind it. None of them would answer him, and even threatening them with suspension, he couldn't get an answer. It wasn't until a woman sat down beside him that the kids, all of them, scattered to the seven winds and disappeared.

"I'm Parker." He asked her why he should care what her name was. "Because if you don't resign from your position as principal of the high school here, I'm going to make your life a scoop of rocky road with nuts. I'm going to be using your nuts, by the way, when I put the cherry on top of your head."

"I haven't the slightest idea what you're talking about. I will not resign from my position, nor will I allow you to threaten me in such a manner." Parker told him she never once threatened him. "You did too. While I don't fully understand what you were saying you were going to do to me, I did understand it to mean you were going to harm me in some way."

"I was making you a promise, shithead. I don't make threats. You either do things the way I want them done, or I scoop you up with my magic and hurt you in places you'd never thought of before. Resign or be hurt. It's really that simple."

Clyde turned his back to her and looked out over the empty football field. He didn't know what was going on with that, but he had a feeling some of it was due to this woman beside him. Her laughter had him turning toward her again.

"You have no idea what sort of shit I can rain down on you, do you? Well, that's all right too. I have lots of information now that I didn't before. You really think you're some sort of slick shit, don't you? I mean, who would have thought you'd have kids paying out for uniforms you had hopes of getting donated? By the way, Brook isn't going to donate shit while you're still acting like you run this place. She couldn't write it down without several hundred curse words, so her husband wrote it for her. I don't know if there are any fewer curse words in the note you have there, but it's probably more coherent." He wasn't worried about Brook and her husband. They'd fall into place too. Clyde decided not to give the woman anything more to talk to him about. "Don isn't going to be blackmailed either. You should have asked him to come and help out. He would have done it willingly. Don is a good teacher and well liked around here. In case you're wondering, that's why none of the kids are going to be playing this year. So your plans of making a killing off the concession stand as well as the football camp and uniforms aren't going to fly. People don't like you."

"I have no idea what you're talking about." She just grinned at him. For some reason, he was afraid of her. She looked — Well, she looked evil. "Go back to whatever you were doing and leave me to my work. I don't know if you actually know Don Foster or not, but he'd better be showing up here, or he's going to be out of a job. As for Brook, she'll pay for the uniforms, and more than likely even allow me to have a little extra for the band when I'm finished with her. She isn't that good with money. Have you seen how much she spends on advertising? Why I ask you? She has more work now than she could possibly get finished. I don't know how smart she's supposed to be, but to me, that just shows a lack of any kind of intelligence."

"Are you telling me you think Brook is stupid?" Clyde told the woman if the shoe fit, then yes, he was saying that. "That's really too bad of you. From what I've been able to figure out about Brook, she's really smart. I mean, she did start that company all on her own. Not to mention all the money she has made over the years. I think—and this is just me and about every other person in this town—she's brilliant."

"Yes, well, you've not shown a great deal of intelligence either, now have you?" The woman just laughed. "What are you doing here? To tell me that I'll not have Brook eating out of my hand? I will. And that brother-in-law of hers too. I know how much he wants to coach football. He has often made known to me his need to be a part of it. So what if it's my plan to make a little cash on the side? It's not as if I'm paid all that well anyway. I'm not hurting anyone by trying to make myself a better retirement. To have a little extra on my plate when I sit down to dinner. They'll do what I want because I want them to. And since you've no say in any of this, I'd appreciate it if you would just go about your own business and leave me alone."

"Let me get this straight in my mind. You're going to make Brook Foster donate enough money to not only supply the football team with new uniforms but also put something extra in your pocket. And if that wasn't enough for you, you're going to skim the profits off the concession stands to— What did you say? Oh yes—put a little extra on your plate. Sorry to tell you this, but you look as if you've had too much on your plate already. Perhaps you should have invested in a rowing machine or a treadmill. Anyway. On top of the Brook donations, you plan on blackmailing Donahue Foster into coaching the football team by telling him if he doesn't do what you want, you'll simply fire him as a teacher. That's not particularly nice of you, is it?" He told her he didn't care what she thought. "No, I can see you don't. Back to your plans. Since the parents of the teams, as well as the band members, donate most of the food, as well as their time in working the stand, you plan on taking a portion of their profits as well. Quite a little money maker you have going on here, isn't it?"

"As I said to you before, I don't make a great deal of money. And why wouldn't I want to make this a profitable thing for myself? I am the one making sure things work in my favor." He smiled at her, just thinking of a great comeback to her. "It's not as if all the money is going to me. I'm only skimming some of the profit from the stand. The money for the uniforms isn't going anywhere else but my bank account. Think of it as taking care that I don't have to be on welfare when I'm finished being the greatest principal of all time. Why I might even write a book about how to do what I've done. It would be a best-seller among people like me. Underpaid principals that need just a little extra."

"I pity you when all this gets out." He asked her how she thought it was going to be out in the public. "What if I told you I was recording all of this?"

Clyde laughed. "First of all, simply recording my voice wouldn't get you anywhere. It would be my word against yours. And I'm a respected member of society." She said he had been one. "No, I am. Only you and I have any idea what is being said here. And as I pointed out, no one would believe you anyway."

"Did I mention that I am magical? I'm sure I did. It's one of the things I shared with my husband to be, Donahue Foster. People think we're married, but we're mated, so it's all the same. But I digress. Being magical, I was able to get you to just sit here and confess everything you've been up to without much in the way of encouragement." He asked her what that had to do with anything. "A great deal, as a matter of fact. If you look out over the bleachers here, you'll begin to see why the kids disappeared. They're not adults, and although I didn't have your permission, it matters little since I didn't ask you for any kind of information on your crimes. Is what I hid from you beginning to show yet, Clyde?"

He didn't see anything on the field, nor in the bleachers. Just as he was turning to her, to ask this person what she was talking about, he saw the local news station there with a video camera pointed directly at them. As he continued to look, he saw that not only was there the local news, but it looked like there were people from several different news organizations as well, and a lot of other people. People looking terribly upset with the things he'd said.

Thinking fast had never been his strong suit. He had to make notes and cross out things that he couldn't make work. Turning to Parker again, he smiled as best he could and told her he was kidding about all of it.

"Kidding? I don't know, Clyde. You seemed to have everything worked out pretty well for someone that was just *kidding*. Besides, in addition to coming here and speaking to you about this—by the way, thanks for being so forthcoming—the police and the FBI have been going through your home and your bank accounts. Again, thank you for having all your passwords written down for us. That surely did save us a great deal of footwork." He stared at the crowd of people there in front of them. "They want to talk to you, it seems. But if I were you, I'd just go to the police over there and turn myself in. I think you might be safer in the police's custody than with the people you were trying to scam."

He thought she might be right. Clyde was caught. There wasn't a thing he could do or say to make it better. He was of a mind, just for a moment, to run. But where would he go? he thought. With his picture and his words plastered all over the place, all he could do was go to jail.

"You've ruined everything. You know that, don't you?" Parker asked him how he'd come to that conclusion. "There will be no uniforms for the team. The money for the new stadium I was going to have Garrett Construction donate is now defunct. You've ruined everything that would have made this school great."

"I see. Well, now that you're going to prison — I hope you understand that — but since you're not going to be here to take what didn't belong to you, Brook is donating the money for the new uniforms. Don is going to be the assistant coach for the team. The concession stand has a standing order for not just all the water they want, but there will be hot dogs and any other kind of food they wish to sell there, courtesy of Don and I. Mrs. Foster, Don's mom, is also going to have the party barn ready so the school can use it to host events to try and raise money — free of charge so long as they clean up afterward. If you ask me, I think things are much better than the way you were going to run things. Not to mention, it's all done legally." Clyde asked her what she was getting out of this. "Me? A happy family. My husband doing something he loves, and you gone. I should have started with that one. You being gone from this school means so much to all of us."

As Clyde was being taken away, people started throwing things at him. A tomato hit him in the head. Unpopped popcorn kernels hit him in the face and arms, cutting into his skin. Even the players were bombarding him with footballs, helmets, as well as obviously well-used jockstraps.

The police did nothing, not even when he told them to

help him. As he was put into the back seat of the cruiser, he looked to see a man sitting there as if waiting for him. It took him a moment to realize who it was. Ronan Foster, a big man anyway, looked ginormous sitting there in the seat watching him.

"I know you understand now why you don't fuck with my family." Clyde told him he'd done nothing wrong. "Yet here you sit, handcuffed, in the back of a police cruiser. Don't lie to me again. Do you understand me?"

"What are you going to do about it? Kill me? I don't think so. I don't know if you realize this or not, but there are people out there that think I'm doing a wonderful job as principal." The pop to his face knocked his head back into the window behind him. Blood ran down his face from his nose. "What was that for? I'll sue you for that. See if you don't end up right in the cell next to mine."

"You go on thinking that and we'll see who believes anything that comes out of your mouth. Don't lie to me again." Clyde said nothing. "We've emptied all of your bank accounts. Taken care that the things you purchased with the school funding are on the auction block. Also, and I find this as funny as fuck, all your pretty little porn pictures are now with the FBI. My goodness, Clyde, you've been a very naughty boy, haven't you? Having your pictures and video sent to the school means a big-time prison sentencing. They don't even care that it was sex you were having sent to you. You just shouldn't have used the school's address or, and this one is a biggy, the school's computer to download it."

"I have no idea what you're talking about."

This time when the punch to his face slammed him backward, he heard the window crack. Or it might have been his head. As dizzy as he was, he didn't care which it was. Clyde just wanted it to stop.

There were more questions and two more pops to his face. Laying his head back, Clyde wondered why no one was coming to help him. Then he realized, and it hurt him to think this, no one cared about him. Crying all the way to the jail, he wondered what his mom was going to say about all this. She'd be really testy with him for sure.

~~~

Peter might well have been overwhelmed by the size of the Foster men, but they were so willing to be kind to him; he didn't feel that way for long. Even Mrs. Foster— Jane, he was asked to call her—was so nice he wanted to spend more time with her.

"They're all the family I have left, these kids and their mom. My son, the father of the men here, was a piece of shit, and I'm glad every day that someone took him out of the human race." Peter couldn't help it. A burst of laughter came out. "Yes, I knew you'd find that funny. But he was. Rollin. Why on earth we gave him that ridiculous name is beyond me. He really was an abusive prick, and my lovely granddaughter-in-law killed him. It was us or him, and I'm very thankful she did it for me."

"Was he anything like Park Carter? There is a man I'd like to figure out how to kill again." Jane said they were working that part out. "Yes, I heard. Parker has been going over my books from my family. Wouldn't it be wonderful if you could do like a search on spells? I mean, like put them all in a file and be able to access just what you want at a moment's notice?"

Jane stared at him. Telling her he was sorry if he'd said something wrong, he was shocked when she kissed him on the cheek before yelling for Parker. He didn't know what he'd done, but he'd been paid well for it. He might even try something again, just on the off chance she would do the same thing.

He'd been a widow for a while—eight long years without companionship or anyone he could just sit around the house with and not feel so alone. It was the main reason he'd accepted the dinner invitation so readily. Peter was a lonely old man.

Peter hated to feel sorry for himself. He didn't like it in others and hated it, even more, when he did it. Looking at Parker, who was talking to Jane, he wondered what it would be like to have been around her when Parker had been a child.

You wouldn't have liked me. He stared at his granddaughter for several seconds, wondering how she'd spoken to him. *I'm a witch, remember. Before you warn me about reading people's minds, I will tell you to never play poker. Your face shows just what you're thinking. And you're not lonely but allowing yourself to be alone. There is a difference. Stop feeling sorry for yourself and get up off your ass and talk to people. I can't do everything for you.*

It's been much too long. I haven't any idea how to talk to people face to face. I wouldn't even know how to bring up a conversation that I have any knowledge about. She asked him if he liked animals. *Well, of course, I do — what a silly thing to ask me.*

Not silly at all. The man to your right is Loman Foster. You might not know who that is, but you have several of his photos in your den. He's the photographer that uses a paw print on his pictures. Peter loved the man's work. *Also, there is an attorney in the room with you. Cassidy Foster. People sometimes refer to him as Hop Along, simply because he doesn't waste any time in the courtroom when he is there. I think he holds the record for the quickest divorce case of a celebrity ever.*

As she told him what each of the men in the room did for a living, he realized he was in a room full of greatness. However, Parker warned him that they didn't think of themselves as anything but men doing a good job, just like their mother had told them to do when they were younger and had a task to do.

You'll embarrass them, and while it might be funny to me, not so much to them. My mate, too, is a great man. I knew it before I realized he was my mate, I think. He's one of the only football players in high school to receive the All American award twice in a row, beating out other kids that had played ball long before he decided it would be a cheap way to get into college. He asked what grade he taught. *High school math and science. Don has also helped develop many medical formulas that have helped in the health field.*

And their mother? What has she done? Parker asked him what he meant. *I meant nothing by it. But she has to be one extraordinary person to have raised these men all alone.*

She raised them to be compassionate men that care more for their fellow man than they do themselves. Each of them would willingly do anything for any of their family. Which would include you should you need them. Family is the most important thing to them. Parker laughed a little. *They will die for their mother and grandma. For their mates too. Each and every one of them are men you can be proud to know and call a friend. So again, Grandda, get up off your ass and go figure out what you might have in common with them. Even if you find you have nothing, they'll still be as polite to you as I am rude to you.*

That's a lot of politeness. I mean, even if you'd said half of your rudeness, it would have been a great deal.

They both laughed, and he looked at what was being handed to him. "What's this?"

"You must pay attention to me like Camilla does." He grinned at Jane when she spoke. "Parker did this. It's all on the computer now, just as you said. And the best part of it is, it's easy to access from your phone should you be out and need some spell, or whatever they're called."

He didn't have any idea what she was talking about.

It must have been obvious to everyone because they all started explaining the file that Parker had made on a computer. He was just having things come together when he put in a search for the dead living in the living. They'd let him be the first to use it.

"It says it's not an easy spell to cast on one of the dying. It's easier to use the spell on yourself before you're dead. I would think that was a given." They all laughed as he continued to read the instructions for the spell. "It seems simple enough. There isn't much to it to make the person leave the living. However, if there's nothing else I've learned over the years, it's that nothing is as uncomplicated at it seems." Peter handed the laptop to Parker for her to have a look at.

"It says there mustn't be any blood relations between the witch and the dead. If there is, even if it's a long line of generations between them, the dead can pull the living to them and use their body." Parker looked at him. "I'll need your help with this, even if it's only for support. The two of us together can make it work better than me just going there and yanking him free. I can do that. But it does say it's tricky to do, and the dead can cause all sorts of damage to its host."

"I would gladly help you. But as I told you before, I haven't had an occasion to use my magic all that much since my son was murdered." Parker said he'd do fine. "Thank you. When would you like to do this? It also says that the longer the dead is in the living, the more difficult it is to get him out."

"Eight years." Peter nodded, knowing it had been a long time. "What if we just did this today, before we have dinner with the family? I'd like for you to be able to speak to my mom. Get to know her a little better."

"I'd like that. All we need is room. Between the two of us, I'm thinking we have ample magic. And with the lions here, there will be added support from them as well." Jane asked him how that would work. "Long ago, an uncle of mine told me a secret to making magic stronger. He said, pulling from the shifters that might be around you, which are all magic, will give your magic a boost you might not have even thought about."

It was settled then. Meggie was called to tell her what they were doing, and one of the brothers went to get her. Parker and he went outside to the sunshine and worked on where the best place would be to do this. Peter did warn her she would have to have someplace to put the specter of Park when she pulled him free.

"If you don't, he could find another host to terrorize." She asked him what it could be. "Anything really, so long as it's sealable and can withstand a little abuse. Glass works, or a stone. I've seen both used."

"I can cast him to a stone?" Peter told her how it would work. "So I just pull him free and tell him to go to a stone. How would that seal? I'm not being stupid, but it seems if there was a rock big enough to hold him, it would easily break."

"It could, and actually, it happens a great deal. But you're forgetting something. A stone is nature made. And as a white witch, we rely on the earth more than we do anyone. When you cast him to the stone, it will take him inside of all of it because of what we are. Then, if a single chip is taken from the stone after he's put in it, he can never be released from it. Even if it's ground down to fine sand. He becomes the stone." She grinned at him. "I don't think I like that look. It looks to me as if you're plotting. Are you?"

"I am. But I don't know that I'm going to use the stone at all. It's a good thing to put him into, I think. However, I'd like for him to suffer, and to suffer for the rest of the days, there is an earth for him to be upon. I have a couple of spells I can use that will be as effective as the stone. I don't want him to get off so easily as just being put away. Do you?" Peter decided he never wanted to make this woman his enemy. "You have nothing to worry about, Grandda. I can't hurt you. We're blood-related, and it's against the rules."

He wasn't sure if she was kidding him or she was actually trying to comfort him. It wasn't—comforting. Again, to himself, he vowed never to piss her off. Peter had a feeling she'd kill him slowly and with a great deal of pain if he should harm her in any way. Hurting her new family would be a reason for her to kill. Yes, Peter thought he was going to forever keep on her good side.

They had the wording, and the spell all worked out.

Everyone knew their places, and he was going to be support to her. Don said he'd stand by him, just in the event something went wrong and he could protect him. Peter didn't tell him, but he thought if anything went wrong, they'd all be screwed.

When Meggie showed up, he could tell how worn out she was. Her face was gaunt, and she looked to be exhausted. Right then and there, he decided he was going to take her home with him. The two of them needed each other now. Yes, he thought, he'd have his friendship with the family, and make amends with Meggie for all she'd been put through. It was a good and solid plan, he thought. Also, a way to get Parker and her new family to come and visit them some. He missed having a family and was going to do something about that. Today if he could.

Chapter 7

Park felt himself being torn from his hiding place. Not even being dead was keeping the pain at bay. He knew who it was and why she was doing this, and he wasn't going to do anything she wanted. After reading all the books he had on spells and casting, he knew that as his daughter, she would have to give him what he wanted. And what he wanted was for her to hand herself over to him so he could live again.

Snarling at her when Park pulled halfway from her mother, he saw Parker smile at him. Christ, it was painful when she did that shit. First of all, the sun was much too bright for his tender eyes. Then there was the fact that he couldn't use his magic while he was half in and half out of this body.

As soon as they were finished with this shit, Park was going to kill Meggie. She'd been useless since the day he'd married her. It had bothered him on so many levels that he'd been tricked into wedding her. Perhaps tricked wasn't the correct word, but he'd been something. Her family should have had more power than they did. Park had also thought that since she'd been engaged to a Windchaser, her fiancé would have given all he was to her when he died. Nothing had gone right.

He wouldn't admit this to anyone but himself, but he'd rather enjoyed killing Peter. He was strong. It had been one of the reasons he'd murdered him. But the magic never appeared. Nor did he get any of the jollies one gets when killing a being that is stronger than yourself. It, in addition to the magic, was why he murdered so much. For the jollies. Glaring at Parker when she laughed, he wanted to strangle her right now. If he didn't need her as badly as he did, Park thought he'd do just that.

"Well, you're not looking all that good, are you?" He snarled again at Parker. "Yes, that'll get you some brownie points, won't it? Park, I'm to understand you have a request of me. Go ahead and ask me so that I can turn you down, and we'll get to more enjoyable shit today."

"As my daughter, you have to do as I wish. I demand that you, as my blood daughter, give yourself to me so I may live my life that was cut short." Parker asked him if that was all. "What do you mean is that all? You're not doing anything I demanded of you. You have to do what I tell you."

"Not really. First of all, I hate you. Secondly. I really

loathe you." Park told her he didn't really care. "No, I didn't think you would. However, you've made your demand, and I've refused it. What other things do you wish to say before I take care of you? If nothing, I'd really love for you to be gone."

"You have to do what I tell you." He felt a stirring in Meggie's body. It took him a moment to realize she was laughing. "What are you doing? You've nothing to laugh about, bitch. Did you know that as soon as I'm finished with you, you'll be dead?"

"No. That's not okay with me, either." He told Parker to shut up. The adults were talking. "Yes, well, it might have slipped your mind, but I'm an adult too. I have boobies and everything now. And you're not going to be around long enough to kill anyone. You're going to suffer in ways you never have before since you murdered for the joy of it."

"You think you're all badass, don't you, Parker? Well, you might be powerful, but I'll have you know that you don't know half the magic I do." She asked him what he knew that he thought she didn't. "As my blood relative, I can demand that you hand over what I want. I tried being nice, but you've made it so now I have to take what should have been mine all along."

"You see, right there is where you're wrong. Not just that, but this entire thing about you being able to demand anything of me. I'm not your daughter." He told her she lied. "Nope. Not about this. You see, I'm the daughter of Peter Windchaser, one of the most powerful warlocks ever born. As his daughter, I inherited all that he was when you murdered him. I don't know if you're aware of this or not, but it's looking kind of sucky for you right now. Don't you think?"

He felt a change from Meggie then as if she was suddenly in possession of some kind of magical surge. Turning to look at her, he saw an elderly man holding her from behind like he was going to fuck her or something. He told the man to get away from his wife.

"You've really bitten off more than you can chew, Park." The man laughed. "As father to Peter Windchaser, and grandfather to Parker Foster, I lend my power to Meggie to be able to rid herself of you."

Park screamed at the pain surging into him like volcanic waves. There was little time between one surge to the next. As soon as it stopped, he felt his body weaken more, his magic drained. Pulling back to hide away in Meggie's body, he found that not only was there no room for him, but he also hurt every time he tried. The magic she had been given was pushing him out. It wasn't fair, damn it.

"What have you done to me?" Parker said she'd done nothing. Not yet at any rate. "I demand you stop this right now and be gone with yourself. I'm going to stay here for the rest of her days. There is shit you can do about it either."

"Oh, but you are so wrong on that score."

Taking a step back, Parker lifted her hands into the air. Park could feel the magic as it tightened around him. It was stronger than anything he'd ever felt before. As much as he hated to think about this, the man might have been right. He had bitten off more than he could chew, for this pain was far worse than when he'd been killed.

"Earth, wind, fire, and love of the purest heart, I ask you for your help in ridding this monster from the body of my biological mother."

As he was being ripped from the living part of his wife, he tried his best to hang on. It was horrific, the feelings he was getting. Not just hatred, although there was more than enough of that, but he could feel love too. Parker to Don. Peter to Meggie. Meggie to Parker. There was so much of it he was beginning to be ill from it. Physically, he was sure he couldn't throw up, but his body didn't seem to know that. As he was dry heaving, he felt himself being pulled from his host. The pain was incredible. Park screamed with it.

"Take me." He looked at Parker when she backed away from him. "You must take me. I'm your father."

"I'm glad to say you're not, as I have said to you before. You're not anything to me but an abusive bastard." Rising up, he was weak, his magic all but gone. Reaching for Parker, he encountered a large lion. "I'd like for you to meet my mate, Park. And even though Don cannot touch you until I tell him, he can, however, take the rest of you from Mom. Don, tear him apart."

The lion swiped its paw at him. He felt it as if he were whole again, but only for the second, he was removed completely from Meggie. Several more times, the claws tore through his ghostly body, until he was nothing more than ribbons of himself laying on the ground. Parker and Meggie stood over him, and as he looked up at them, Meggie kicked him hard enough to scatter him to the winds.

"Park Emerson Carter, you are hereby ordered — from now until there is no more earth — to live as you are now. You will have no magic. No one will aide you. Not a witch or other creature will come to you when you call. From this time forward, you will blow along the winds as you are now. Separated from the rest of your parts." Parker grinned at him. "I sentence you to feel each breath that blows over you. Every time a wound happens to you, it will never heal. Each of your parts will know pain, and you shall feel each wound every time you are injured. Get yourself away from here forever."

He watched as he was lifted up by a strong wind. The long strips of his body flew in every direction. As one part of him was knocked against a tree, the rest of him felt it. One part of him was caught in a lawnmower that cut him into smaller pieces that flew again. Dizzying heights made him wish for one more chance. One more bit of magic so he could kill Parker. However, all he did was float upwards, then down. Over things, then on them. Parker had done him wrong. And he was going to make sure, somehow, that she paid him back for all of this ill treatment.

~~~

"Did you read this?" Mae shoved the newspaper in her brother's face. "This says that cheap whore is getting married. We have to warn him. At least see if he can take a bribe and not marry into our family. You know as well as I do that she's not going to amount to anything. Much less marry into anything other than someone like herself."

"Mae, I'm working here." She didn't think putting together a model car was any form of work, and she slammed her hand down on the pieces he'd been painstakingly putting together. "Why would you do that? You know this is the only thing that makes me happy. The one thing I do so I can put up with you as you live in my house. I should knock you into that wall."

"You can try." He picked up the pieces, broken all over the table and floor. "Did you hear a darn thing I said to you? Parker is getting married. Who would marry a slut like her? Not anyone we'd want to have around."

"Since she's never made any kind of move to come around us, I think that's about the most truthful statement you could have made." He shoved the pieces that were still left to break off the plastic holder into the box it had come in this morning. "I haven't any idea why you hate that girl so much anyway. We've never had a thing to do with her or her mother. Also, you never cared for Park.

I've gone along with all this stuff you wanted because I don't want to have to argue with you. But it would be nice if you were to explain to me why you have such a burr up your butt about her."

"I don't explain myself to anyone." She was sure he said he knew that under his breath, but he wouldn't repeat it. "I'm the younger sister, and you both should have listened to me when I pointed out that marrying someone was going to cause you all sorts of bad things befalling you."

"So, you did. However, I'm of a mind that had you not murdered my fiancée, she might have made me incredibly happy. I know being away from you certainly would have." Mae couldn't understand why they just didn't do what she wanted in the first place, and she wouldn't have had to resort to murder. "You go on thinking that. I know for a fact that I'd never been happier than when I met and fell in love with my Alex."

Mae decided to just ignore him for now. She had more important things to do today anyway.

Picking up the phone, she called the newspaper the article was being run in. As soon as the person answered, she knew she was going to have to go down there and show them that the customer was always right.

"I would like to know where this picture was taken." The woman asked her what picture. "The one in my hand, dumb ass. Where was this thing taken? I also want to know the address right now."

"Ma'am, since I'm not there and we're not on a video call, I cannot tell what picture you are speaking about." The girl laughed. "Not that it matters, really. I cannot give you any address that an article might be running from unless it is with the permission of the person we were interviewing."

"I'll wait." Mae sat down at the table she used for a desk when she was on the main floor of this monstrous house. Her desk in her room was neat and orderly. There wasn't even a pencil out of place. "Hello, are you still looking?"

"I'm not sure what you think I should be looking for, ma'am. I've already told you I don't know what picture it is you're talking about." Growling at her made the person laugh. "That doesn't help either. If you don't cooperate with me to help you figure this out, I'm going to hang up."

"You hang up on me, and I'm going to come down there and beat the crap out of you. I swear to Jesus. I've asked you nicely about the picture, now —"

Raymond jerked the phone from her and glared. "You're the stupidest person I know." When he started using his nice voice, one to talk to people other than her, Mae knew he was talking to the girl. "She wants to know where the picture came from of the announcement of Parker Carter and Donahue Foster getting married. I believe it's their engagement picture or something like that."

She couldn't hear what the woman was saying to her brother. She must have said something about her because Raymond looked at her and laughed. The cheeky girl was going to be in trouble if she didn't get her answers. Mae was thinking she'd go there anyway. There was some lesson learning to be done.

"Yes. I understand. I know privacy is an important thing nowadays. I don't suppose it would matter that Parker is our niece?" She must have told him no. He didn't even sound pissed either. "Yes, thank you for being so patient with my sister. She has no manners at all. You have a good day."

When he hung up the phone, she asked him what the address was. He told her he'd not gotten it. Mae wanted to slap that smile off his face when he turned away from her and went back to his chair.

"You should have given the phone back to me if you weren't going to do what I wanted. That girl wouldn't help me at all. I will need that address to warn the young idiot marrying Parker. What sort of name is that anyway? Parker." He told her the same thing he said to her every time she mentioned how stupid the name was. "Yes, I know she was named after Park, but that's not a name for a girl to have. They should have asked me if I approved of it or not. That would have been easier."

"I'm sure, like me, Park didn't give two noodles as to what your opinion was about things that weren't a concern to you. And I'm especially sure he didn't care what you wanted to name his child." Raymond flicked the newspaper as if he was trying to irritate her. "Just leave them alone, Mae. If you don't, you're going to be put in jail again, and you can be sure I'm not going to be making my way down there to bail you out. It's not fair of you to bother someone that hasn't done a thing to either of us."

"Not done anything to us? That woman killed our brother." He said she'd not. That was why they let her go. "She did too kill him. I don't care what the officer said to me. Did you know they paid her for lost wages when she left the prison? That money should have come to us."

Raymond looked at her. "Why on earth do you think that money should have come to us? It's not as if we spent any time in jail with her. I'm telling you right now, Mae. Just back off and leave her alone." She slammed her hand down through his newspaper. "What the heck was that for? You know this is one thing I enjoy before dinner."

"Well, now you can't do it. You're to march down there right now and find out where they live. I don't care if you have to be there all night." He picked up the paper she'd shredded and ignored her. "Did you hear me? I am not in the best of humor, Raymond. That man needs our help, and I plan on giving it to him."

"I'm not marching anywhere, Mae. I'm sixty-three years old, and I'm finished with walking anywhere." He wadded up the paper and put it neatly into the trash can. "What is your beef with them? You've never allowed me to have a thing to do with the child or her mom. Never once have we sent her a birthday or holiday card. Now that she's getting married and is probably happy—and I'm happy for her—you want to get all up in her Kool Aid and mess things up for her. Just don't, Mae. Leave her to her own self and stay the heck away from her."

"Did you want to screw her too?" Raymond leaned back in his chair and didn't answer her. "That's it, isn't it? You want to have sex with her. That's why every holiday you ask me if we should send her something. I knew it."

"You don't know anything. She's my niece. What makes you think those kinds of sick things?"

Mae knew that was what he wanted. It was what all men wanted. Well, she would put a stop to that too.

Raymond stood up. "I'm going to take a walk. When I return, we can go and get some dinner. But not if you're in this mood. I'll go myself. I don't know where your head is sometimes."

"It's right here on my shoulders, you old fool." Raymond was out the door before she could ask him where he was going. Taking a walk? He just told her he didn't want to walk. "He's going to do what I wanted. He's headed there right now to get me the address."

Going to her room, she found a suitable dress to wear out with her brother. They had dinner out weekly, and she tried extremely hard to make sure she was dressed well each time. He would more than likely put up a fuss about what she was wearing, as he did every time. But it was her responsibility to make sure the Carter name was one to be proud of. As she pulled her dress over her head, she thought of Parker.

It wasn't really the child she hated. It was Park for not asking her if he could marry. Of course, he would have done as he wanted and not have minded at all what her opinion was. But it was the fact that he'd not asked her at all. Mae looked at the dress in the long mirror and hated the color. Running her hands down the lilac dress, it was a nice soft shade of brown when she finished.

Raymond had the lion's share of the magic that had been passed down from their parents. She supposed with him being the oldest, that was the way it should have been. But she begrudged him for it. He didn't even use it all that much. He'd repair a button off his shirt or coat. Put on a pair of boots if the weather turned. Small things he'd do in front of her just to make her upset. Never once had he ever done anything fun with it. Mae had only ever been able to change the color of whatever she was wearing. It was a lame bit of magic. She couldn't even change her clothing to something fun. No, she'd been left out of something better.

Even Park had more than her. He'd been born after her, and he'd still gotten a bit more than her. It wasn't fair. It was like she'd been singled out, and now she had to suffer because she had nothing to fall back on.

As soon as she heard the front door open, Mae made her way down the stairs. She was nearly to the front hall when she saw the young woman standing there. It was Parker and some man. Brice, their butler, had let them in.

"What are you doing here?" Parker looked at her, and she could see something different about her. Not that she could tell from where she was standing, but it looked like she'd tatted herself all up. "Just like the whore that you are. First thing you do when you get some money is mark up your body like some sort of hobo."

"I doubt very much that a hobo could afford to get tatted up, as you called it. But this came to me today. I got it from my grandda." Mae told her she didn't have any grandparents. "Then how did my parents come to be in this world without them having parents?"

Mae hadn't any idea what she was saying, so she ignored it in favor of coming down the rest of the stairs. When she was level on the floor with Parker and the man, she realized how tall she was. No one in her family was over five foot six or seven. Trying to stretch herself to be as tall, she nearly fell off her heels.

"I've come to let you know that Park is no longer going to be bothering anyone." Mae asked her what she'd done. "So you did know he was living in my mother. I thought as much. You didn't seem all that upset when you were told he was dead."

"You killed him again, didn't you? What was he supposed to do but find a way to live again, after the way he was treated by your mother? Why isn't he with you? He told me that was the way the magic would work for him." Parker told her he'd messed with the wrong woman. "I suppose you think it was you. Your mother wasn't anything but a sap. Why she ever agreed to marry Park is beyond me. If I'd had anything to do with it, you would never have been born."

"I'm not Park's child. So your prediction on that is all off." Mae told her she was a liar. "Why is it when someone doesn't agree with a fact you're giving them, they immediately start out by calling the person a liar? I'm not. I'm the daughter of Peter Windchaser. My mom was pregnant with me when Park killed Peter. Mom didn't consent to marry him either. He forced her hand by going to the witches' council and them making her wed him to create a pure witch child. I was too much for Park, it seems, as I was able to not only take him from my mom but to make sure he suffered for as long as the earth turns."

"Why are you saying these things? I want you to tell me the truth." Parker said she was, that she had no reason to lie to her. "But you are. You were nothing to me and my brother."

"That, Mae, is the whole truth and nothing but the truth. I'm not related to either of you." The door opened, and there stood Raymond. He was a little damp— it looked as if he'd showered in his clothing. "Hello, Raymond. I came to tell you both that Park is now out of my mom, and that I'm no relation to either of you."

"I knew the relationship part. I've known that since you were born." He looked at Mae, and she asked him what he was talking about. "I told you all along that Parker wasn't our niece. I only went along with you to keep the peace here. Are you ready for dinner?"

"I am, but I want her to tell me the truth." Neither of them said anything to her. But Raymond did ask them if they wanted to join them for dinner. "I will not break bread with that whore and her whatever he is."

"Careful, Miss Carter. I'm not like your brothers. I will take a bite out of you that will make you understand I won't tolerate you treating Parker this way." She asked the man what he was talking about. Instead of answering her, the man shifted to a great lion. Then he was a man again. "I'll tear you apart without any thoughts as to how messy it will be in this lovely house."

"Did you see that, Raymond? He's a monster. Kill him." Raymond turned to the young man and put out his hand. She slapped it away and told him again to kill him. "He's a monster."

"He's no more a monster than I am. You are, however. So I was thinking if anyone gets killed for being a monster, it should be you." He turned to the couple. "Would you like to have dinner with me? Since Mae has decided to decline, I'd love to have a nice quiet meal with the two of you."

Mae couldn't believe it when they both agreed. Then,

before she could tell them they were not leaving this house, she was left alone standing in the hall, like her prom date had done all those years ago.

Surely they would return for her. As she stood there waiting, tapping her foot to make sure she was doing it when Raymond returned, Mae heard the car start up and then the crunch of gravel as they pulled out of the drive. Looking out the window, she was shocked to see them pulling around the curve of the drive in a long black limo.

Mad now, as mad as she'd ever been, she called for Brice. "I want you to pull the car around for me and take me to where my brother and that trollop is." He asked her where that might be. "Where they went to have dinner. What is wrong with everyone today? Why do I have to explain everything to everyone?"

"Did he tell you where he was going to dinner?" She stomped her foot at him and told him he was getting on her nerves. "As you are mine, Miss Mae. If you don't know where they are, it would be impossible for me to take you there. Unless, of course, you want me to drive you around town looking for his car."

"They were in a limo. What does it matter what they left here in? You'll do as you're told and take me there. I have a few things I want to say to my brother." Brice just turned and left her standing there. "You had better be getting the car for me. I said you're to take me where they are, and I won't be put off again."

Forty minutes later, she was no closer to going to give

her brother a piece of her mind than she was before he left—the nerve of some people. Brice didn't come to her when she yelled for him. It took Mae another half hour to figure out where the kitchen was in the house. She'd never in her life been there.

The place was empty of anyone. There was no food in the pantry that she knew how to cook—nothing in the refrigerator for her to snack on. Even getting a glass of water was impossible for her, as she couldn't reach the cabinets to pull a glass down.

Tomorrow Mae was going to start laying down the law about things. Why she'd not done it sooner was something she asked herself all the time. First thing, she was going to fire Brice and the rest of the staff. Then she remembered the last time she'd done that, and Raymond had hired them back. It was his home, he'd told her, left to him by their parents. Mae was shafted again, she realized. Well, she'd make sure someone knew she was upset. Going to her room, she sat at her table and began making notes. She did so much better when she had notes.

"I'll show them." She made herself three pages of notes before she realized how hungry she was. "I'm not going to put up with this," she yelled to the room. Tomorrow was going to mean big changes for her. They'd better known to follow her rules or else.

Chapter 8

Don was beginning to like the older gentleman. He was cordial to people, even waitstaff, which was a surprise after spending those few minutes with his sister. Ordering a large appetizer for the table, Raymond looked at him as they waited for their food to be brought to them.

"Mae hates appetizers. I think they're the most fun part of the meal. Sort of a precursor for things to come." He laughed a little. "I'm sorry about Mae. I'd like to tell you she's not always like that, but sadly, she is. I usually just go along with whatever she's saying, then do as I want. But lately, since Park got out on his own, she's been meaner. More demanding."

"Why? I mean, why does she hate Parker and Meggie so much?" Raymond told him he wished he knew, but Mae didn't like anyone. Ever. "I see. So even the two of you have been in her line of anger."

"You have no idea. As I said at the house, I knew

Parker couldn't have been Park's. He couldn't have children. He and I shared mumps that sterilized him. I came out of it all right, but then Mae killed my wife to be. Alex would have, I think, made me incredibly happy." They both told him they were sorry. "I am as well. But as I can't do anything about it now, I want to get to know the two of you better. I know some about you. Also, before you find out from someone else, Parker, I arranged for someone to look deeper into your case to get you set free. My thinking was that if Park had forced your hand, he deserved it. It was, I hate to admit, easier to get you out than I thought it would have been. I should have looked sooner than I did. It was about six months ago I had them check, and they released you shortly after. Someone should have done it years ago. Or better yet, at your trial. I'm sorry for waiting so long to help you."

"Thank you for that." Parker put her hand over the young man's. The sigil was there for him to view. She smiled when he was caught staring at it. "It's not a tat, as she said, but something the elements gave me. I know I said it was from my grandda. I just didn't want to have to explain it to anyone that was going to toss me to the side of the road. They marked us both."

When she pulled her small jacket off, Don pulled his dinner jacket off as well and rolled up his sleeve. Raymond was amazed at not just the colors of the sigil, but also how detailed it was. He asked if he could touch it.

"Of course." Parker, using Don's arm, told him what he was seeing. "The vine moves up his spine to the back of his neck. But only on the right side. Mine is only on the right as well. There are flowers on it all the time. They sort of change out depending on where we are, I think. When the two of us left home to come here, the flowers were lilacs, blue and pink ones. Now they look like begonias."

"They're on both your right sides, you said. Do you know why?" Don told him he hadn't any idea, while Parker told him she'd not been able to look into it. "I know why. It's so when your backs are together, you form a whole. Whole what, I don't know. But I'd bet, like the flowers, it changes with whatever you need it for. It's supposed to be enormously powerful magic when the two halves make a whole."

Their appetizer plate was brought to them, and Don waited to pull what he wanted from it last. Honestly, he didn't know what some of the things were. Raymond seemed to understand this and explained the parts of it to them as he filled a plate for not just him, but Parker as well.

Enjoying the rib bites and the deep fried ravioli, Don told Raymond what he did for a living. Raymond, at one time, had been a teacher as well. He'd taught history. Don told him he should do it again.

"You know, I've thought of it several times. If you want to know the truth, I'm sick of doing the same thing every day. It was something I thought of when Mae destroyed a model car I was working on." He laughed again. "I do it to relax. If I were any more relaxed, I'd be dead, I think. With Mae around, it's not easy, but I have found my way around her too."

"I thought you'd be upset with me about Park." Raymond asked Parker why she'd think that. "I don't know. You always struck me as an uptight asshole that didn't want things to change you out of your asshole-ness."

Raymond laughed. Don realized the man had a good laugh. It was jolly like you'd hear from a heavy man. Joyful, Don realized. It was a joyful sound. His face reddened when Raymond told him it was joyful to be around them.

"I'm sorry." Raymond told him not to be. "I forget I'm around people that can and will read my mind if I'm not careful."

"I don't usually do it. I'd almost forgotten I could. There hasn't been a great deal to find humor in for a while now. I didn't want you to think I was out for anything other than a good friendly meal with good company. Tell me about yourselves." Don laughed and asked him how much he wanted to know. "Everything you're willing to share. I know a little about the two of you, as I mentioned. Mostly just nonpersonal things. I want to be—I don't know, perhaps an aging uncle or something along those lines. If you don't want any kind of relationship with me, I can and will understand."

"I want to get to know you." Don looked at Parker when she spoke. "My mother, however. I don't want you to harm her verbally or physically as you get to know us."

"I would never do anything to harm your mother in any way. She's...well, she has a special place in my heart. I've always admired her, from a distance, of course. Mae would have done something terrible to her if she'd known. Meggie did a spectacular job in raising you. You're brave, smart, and one of the nicest people I've met." Don asked him if he was in love with her. "I'll be honest with you and tell you I believe I have been, for most of the time she's been Park's wife. You've no idea how many times I wanted to save her from him. But as I said, I think she is only alive now because Mae never knew about it."

"You should see her. Ask her out." Raymond said he'd keep it to himself, as he wished they would as well. "Why? You only have a single life, Raymond. And I believe you could make her happy. I don't think she's been happy for an exceptionally long time. Both of you deserve happiness after all you've been through."

Raymond looked at Parker. It occurred to him that Raymond would love to pursue a relationship with Meggie. However, he'd not do it unless he had Parker's blessing. When she put her hand over his, Raymond took it to his cheek and cried a little. That was all it took for the man to look as happy as he'd ever been, Don would bet.

The rest of their dinner was fun. The meal was wonderful, as was the conversation. Getting to know the older gentleman was very enlightening. He'd had a terrible life too. Mostly due to his parents and sister and brother. Park, it seemed, had been held since he was born.

"He and Mae would cause such trouble when they were in school. Mae dropped out the day she turned sixteen. Park was asked not to return after he failed each year after he was out of elementary school. They told my parents he was just too old." Raymond laughed. "He was forever getting into trouble for trying to date the teachers for a better grade. I say date because I honestly don't think it occurred to him to try sex. He was that stupid. Mae? Well, as you've heard, she doesn't think anyone is as smart as she is. She also expects people to know just what she's speaking about when she asks vague questions of a person. It's annoying to have her around."

"How will you get around to seeing my mom with her around? I don't want anything to happen to her." Raymond told Parker he didn't either. "She'll try and hurt her. We both know that. My mom is an immortal, the same as we are. But she can still be harmed."

"I'm not evading the question, but I would like to see if your mom would have anything to do with me first. You can rest assured nothing will happen to her if we can make a go of it. I'll have Mae committed again if I have to." Don perked up, hearing that. He asked Raymond why she'd been in lock up before. "She's unable to live on her own. Mae thinks she's staying at my home to outlive me so she can live there alone. After she killed Alex, I had to do something with her. I couldn't be around her for exceptionally long periods of time without wanting to murder her myself. She was tested, and immediately they put her into a prison-like setting for the criminally insane. Mae got out because she fooled them all into thinking she was better."

"She's not." Raymond shook his head at him. "I don't know what your plans are for your sister, but I'd think she'd be safer in lockdown. Not just for my mother-in-law's safety, but for you as well. Mae doesn't strike me a someone who would give up easily."

"Oh, you can go to the bank on that. Mae hasn't ever been one to give up easily. I'm betting right now she's asking herself what she's done to be left at home all alone. Or, and this might be more true, she's trying to get one of the staff to take her where we are. It won't matter to her that they might not know where we've decided to dine. She'll just expect her wishes to be taken care of." Parker said she was off her nut. "Truer words have never been spoken. But I will have no issues in getting her put in a home. I've had just about all I can take of her as it is. I don't want to sound cruel, but I'm on my last nerve with her."

When their bill was brought to them, Raymond insisted on paying it. "You don't have to do that,

Raymond. We were already planning to have dinner out anyway."

"It's my pleasure, as a matter of fact. I have to admit, I've not had such an enjoyable time in a very long time. I'd love to do this more often if you don't mind. Even if Meggie turns me down flat, I'd love to continue to get to know the two of you and see how you're doing." Parker told him she'd love that. Then she asked him to dinner tomorrow night. "I'm assuming you want only me to come?" He laughed when they both said yes at the same time. Then Parker spoke again.

"My mom lives with us right now, and I do want you to talk to her. I think between the two of you, you could have a nice life." Raymond said he'd like that. Perhaps he'd sell off his home and move closer. "Yes, well, this twenty-five-minute drive from our home to yours is such a heartache for us."

"I was hinting, to be honest. I said I knew where you lived, but all I knew for sure was that it was in this state." They were headed out the door as Raymond spoke. "To know that you're close enough for me to visit makes me happy too."

Don and Parker were on their way home when his cell phone rang. It was Raymond. He didn't sound stressed or anything when he said hello, but what he had to tell them made Don ask the driver to turn around on the road and head to the house.

"Mae is dead. It looks as if she slipped coming down

the stairs and broke her neck. She's just lying there with her neck all twisted up. It's her shoes. I hated that she felt she had to wear heels. I don't know what to do now." Parker told him they'd be right there. "I've called the police. I just—I guess I shouldn't have called you. I feel silly now."

"You did the right thing, Raymond. You just stay where you are, and we're on our way." Raymond thanked them and asked if they were close. "Yes, we've turned around and are headed toward you right now. Don't worry, Raymond. We'll take good care of you."

When they pulled into the drive, there were several cruisers behind and in front of his car. Moving out of the way of them, Parker got out of the car and made her way to Raymond. Since he knew a couple of the police officers that had worked with his brother, Don stopped to ask them what they knew. He made sure they knew that Raymond had spent a lovely evening with them at dinner and that Mae had been left at home.

"She fell. We can tell it wasn't a murder." He asked him what had happened that made him sure about that. "There are indoor cameras in the house. One of them is on the front door, as well as one on the staircase. Ms. Carter had her hands full when she was coming down the stairs. When it looked like a glass began to slip from her grip, her shoes twisted her up, and she went tumbling down. I'd say she was dead before she hit the bottom here. It's a real shame too. Poor old thing."

Don didn't say anything about him feeling bad about the old bat. Instead, he asked Roger if he could take Mr. Carter to his home tonight so that he wouldn't have to stay in the house. After he was given permission, Don reached out to Parker to ask Raymond to pack some things so they'd take him home. They'd help him take care of the arrangements in the morning.

The car ride was quiet, with only Raymond crying off and on. Parker held Don's hand as they were headed to their home. Don squeezed it tightly when she told him how much she loved him. Don wondered what the elderly man would do now.

~~~

Quin was just entering the grocery store when he saw the man across the street, causing trouble. Anna had been in his offices earlier and had pointed out that her father was in town. It didn't take him long to make sure that Brook had been warned to keep Shirley safe and for him to get Anna to his parents' house. They were more than happy to have her.

"Hey, you. I'm looking for my wife and little girl. I was told they were around." Quin asked him who told him that. "Why does it matter to you, slick boy? I'm here looking for them, and I want someone to tell me where they are."

"I haven't any idea who they are, so I doubt very much I can help you." Taking the cart from the back of the line, he made his way to the produce section. The man followed him, talking to him about his wife and daughter. "I've already told you I don't know them. What do you want me to do for you? Make them appear? I can't. That's not something I would do anyway."

"So you do know where they are." Quin ignored him for a good smelling cantaloupe. When it was slapped out of his hand, Quin let enough of his lion go to show the man he wasn't one to fuck with. "Look at you. Not even a human. What the hell have you done with my wife and child? You'd better know I won't be fucked with on this. They're mine."

"Good for you." Turning his back on the man was all he could do. Killing him, right here in the grocery store, wasn't an option. Well, it was, but not at the moment. The place was busy, and he didn't want anyone to get hurt. Especially not himself. He had a lot of appointments in the morning.

"Hey, pussy face, did you call the cops yet? Seems to me that's what you rich and stupid do when you're faced with someone bigger and meaner than you."

It was getting more and more difficult to ignore the man. After putting a few other groceries in his cart, Quin made his way to the front. Someone had called the police, but it hadn't been him. Along with the two officers, his big brother Ronan was there with Loman. He wondered if his name had brought them both to the store.

"You okay?" Quin said he was, and started pushing his cart toward the checkout line. Ronan stopped him. "I got two calls today from the police. One about the woman that was supposed to have been Parker's aunt — she fell down the stairs and died. The second one was that you were in the store being harassed. If you don't need me, I'm to pick up some steaks for dinner and have you come to our house."

"I haven't any idea why, but he's been harassing me since I got here. I was going to just pick up a few things and head out. But he targeted me the moment I walked in. I wonder what happened there?" Ronan pointed out it might be because he was the only single male in the store. "So you think he thinks I'm with his ex-wife. She's a wonderful person, but she's not my mate."

"I didn't think so. You would have mentioned that when you asked Brook to hire her. By the way, she's working out well." Quin thought she would have anyway. "We're going to get some steaks and bread to have too. What do you think Anna would like to eat? I was also going to slap some chicken on the grill. To have as leftovers later in the week."

"Who the hell are you?" Ronan grinned. "For that matter, what are leftovers? You know as well as I do, there won't be anything even remotely big enough to save in a butter dish, much less for a meal later in the week. I think you've been hanging out with Grandma too much. She saves everything. Did I tell you I was over there the other day, and she was cutting buttons off an old shirt? Why? I asked her, and she said she might need them. For what?

I've never seen her sew a button on anything. Women are weird."

"She got onto Brook the other day when she tossed out a couple of my old shirts. Something about saving the zipper tabs. As far as the leftovers are concerned, I think a man can try, can't he? I sort of like getting up in the middle of the night and finding a hot dog or something in the fridge to eat. Anyway, I don't mess with Grandma. She's hanging out with Brook too much." They were both laughing when Loman asked if he could get some shrimp. "That sounds really good too."

By the time they had filled his cart with extras, things that sounded good to them, Quin was shocked to see that the bill came to just over four hundred dollars. It reminded him to never shop with these two when they were hungry. The police were still speaking with David Harper as they were bagging up their purchases. Quin noticed that Ronan bought flowers for Brook. Both he and Loman bought some for Grandma and Mom, respectively.

As Quin was moving by David, his brothers behind and in front of him, the idiot took a swing at him. David hit him in the face, knocking his bag out of his hand and onto the floor. He didn't even think about the people around but shifted to his cat and pounced on David.

He didn't kill him, not yet anyway. Donny came to kneel down on the floor by their heads. The first thing Donny asked was if Quin was going to press charges.

Ronan answered for him. Yes, he was fucking going to press charges.

"Now, here is what I see with this situation you have yourself in, Mr. Harper. If you move the wrong way, you're going to die. If you try and hurt any of the people standing here, you're going to die. If you so much as curse at either of us when I'm trying to help you—well, I think you know that you're going to die." Donny looked around, then back at Quin and David. "You see, not only do you have a big old lion at your throat, but there are four guns pointed at your noggin right now. Two from my officers, as well as two from very nice citizens that don't want one of their own hurt. I'm going to ask Quin here, real nice like, if he'll let you up, and you'd better be behaving yourself. 'Cause in case you don't know it, bullets come out of a gun really fast. But not as fast as Quin here will have your throat ripped out. And there ain't no coming back from having no throat. You'll be gushing blood like you got yourself plenty to have spraying out of you. You're as good as dead, again, if you do have that happen to you. So, are you gonna behave? Oh yeah, you blink once if you think you can behave until we get you out of here. Or two times if you're stupid enough to think you might survive the next few seconds."

Quin bit down harder when David blinked several times. Donny shook his head and said there wasn't no helping some people. When Donny stood up, Ronan took his place. Ronan, Quin knew, didn't suffer fools very well. He might even kill David before he could. That would really suck, he thought. Ronan would do it just to keep him safe.

"Now you listen here, you fucking piece of shit. I don't care if you blink a hundred times. You fuck up when Quin lets you go, and I'll kill you myself. There isn't any reason whatsoever for you to have touched him."

Quin growled when he felt the gun at his belly. Telling his brother about it, Quin was shoved off of David just as the gun went off, and someone fired at the man on the floor. Quin, as his lion, still just lay there as David cursed and talked about how he was going to sue each and every one of them for shooting him in the arm. It wasn't until Loman stepped up that David not only shut up but paid hard attention to him. Quin thought that Loman having a switchblade at David's balls was doing the trick where the others hadn't been able to.

"You want me to neuter you, you mother fucker?" David shook his head hard, screaming when the knife nicked his inner thigh. "I want to go home with my brothers and have a nice fucking meal. You're fucking that up for me. Now, the police are going to arrest you, and if I hear one word from you while they're doing it, I swear to you I'm going to have your dick and balls in my hand before you can blink."

Quin took his body back, thrilled beyond words that he could be dressed when he went from lion to man. Also that he was going to be here for this. No one would have believed this of Loman.

"He's got my wife." Loman looked at Quin when David pointed at him. Shaking his head, Quin heard Loman tell David he didn't lie. "I heard she was with some pretty boy. He's too pretty to like women, but I thought he might know about her."

"You got your answer. Several times, I'm thinking. Right?" The knife cut him a second time, and now David was sweating. "You hear me?"

"Yes. Yes, I got my answer. Please don't cut me again."

Loman stood up, but not before hitting David in the balls with the end of the knife. As David lay there moaning and crying about the pain, Loman handed Quin the knife. The quietest, most laid back person he'd ever known had handled the situation better than his lion had.

"I was going to give it to you for your birthday. I'm sorry I had to use it before you did."

Quin started laughing. He didn't know what else he was supposed to do, but he laughed harder when the rest of the people around started laughing too. "I guess this was completely out of character for me."

"It was. But I can't thank you enough for it. You did something none of us could." Loman nodded, then moved out of the store. Ronan looked at Quin and just shook his head. "We should remember that. Loman isn't as laid back and in control as we thought. He's scary when pushed."

"Yes, I'd say that is about right." Ronan asked him if he was ready to go. "I mean, we've got all this food. We're not going to let this ass ruin it for us, are we?"

"No. Not at all." Quin looked around, then back at his brother. "She's safe, isn't she? I mean, Shirley, she's at your house and safe, right?"

"She is. Mom has Anna, so she's all right too. We're going to have to talk to the police about this. Neither one of the girls are safe with him running around. They won't be able to hold him for very long." Quin said he knew that, but it would be better if they could. "Don't be like that. You know as well as I do that Donny is doing a good job. He will have my vote in the fall."

"Mine too. But I worry about those other two. What do you suppose happened there between them?" Ronan said he'd bet it was abuse. "I was thinking that as well. Anna is certainly a well-adjusted little girl. Almost too grown up for her age."

After loading up the car, they found Loman taking pictures of some of the old shelving in the back of the store. To Quin, that was all it was, just some old crap that hadn't been picked up by the trash company yet. However, he knew that once he developed the pictures and showed them to him, Loman would have a work of art that would make him wonder why he'd never seen it when he was looking at it. Loman was the best at what he did, and there were, he knew, a great many awards to prove it. He doubted anyone else would know that. Loman, until today, had been very quiet about nearly everything he did.

By the time they got to Ronan's home, all the others had shown up. Even Mom was there, making her famous mustard potato salad. Grandma was making ambrosia salad, and the others were chipping in where they could. It was family time, the kind he enjoyed most of all. Nothing planned, no begging people to come over. Just them, eating and enjoying each other's company.

Chapter 9

Don watched the players as they ran drills. Three days ago, he had been given the notebook that was used by the previous coach for football practice. After going over it twice, he decided he wanted to do his own thing. Have some fun with the kids.

He had three assistants working with him. It had taken him most of the morning to get them to open up to him. Don wasn't sure what had been going on, but now he had their full attention and support. It had taken one of the kids almost passing out on them to get them in his corner.

Robby Gold had been running back and forth on the field. Twice he'd stopped to rest, and the third time, he fell forward on his face. Sitting up, he started to rise again, but Don pushed him back to the ground, telling him to stay put. Then he asked someone to call an ambulance.

"I can do it, Coach. I don't want you to think I'm a

loser." He asked him why he'd think that. "Because I'm sitting down on the job. I can get up and go at it again. I just needed a little breather."

"I don't have any idea why you'd assume I'd call you a loser when it's obvious you're hurting. Just sit where you are, and we'll get you looked over. It might be nothing at all. But then again, it might be something serious. When you're struggling, Robby, you have to tell me. I don't want any of you trying to do more than you should out here in this heat."

Don stayed with the kid until the ambulance arrived. After making sure he was in good hands, he turned to the rest of the team. "It's nearly ninety degrees today. The humidity is high, and you're working hard. If at any time you need to get a drink, do it. If you see a teammate struggling, you should get them to rest. This is our first practice of the season. The first time we're out in the heat dressed in pads. It's too much for me, and I'm not doing half the stuff you are. We're never going to get to the playoffs if you're forever worried I'm going to think you're a loser because you need a minute to adjust. Understand?"

They all nodded, but it wasn't until they took Robby to the hospital to make sure it wasn't anything more than overheating that they began to believe he wasn't going to punish them for anything. And it was after Robby was taken away that things with his assistants got better.

Roger Mason came to stand by him when Robby was

gone. He didn't say anything at first, but once he began speaking, it was as if he'd been bottling up his piece for some time. Don, it just so happened, learned a great deal from the man.

"Billy Wagner, your predecessor, was a bastard. Not only did he make the kids keep pushing themselves beyond what they should have been doing, but he would make fun of them when they did. We lost more players last year because they couldn't handle the hard road he was making them travel than we did to seniors going on to college over a four year period." Don asked him what he would have done to Robby. "Called his dad here, cussed out the kid in front of his father, then made him do several hundred jumping jacks until he 'learned his lesson.' The only lesson any of them learned was that football wasn't any fun, and they didn't want to be beaten to death for it."

"If we don't get a few more players, there won't be a team this year. Did you know that coming here today?" Roger said he was hoping once word got out he was coaching, more would show up. "I hope so. And I want them to have fun at this. They've not won a championship in nearly fifteen years. I had a little idea as to why, but now that you've confirmed it, I guess we'll have to work harder at giving them support rather than a hard time."

"I'm all for that. I was only here today to see what you're like. I know you as a teacher. You taught my daughters math and science. Made it seem like an essential part of growing up. Carol is going to college to become a scientist, and Rae is studying to be a teacher like you. You're a good man, Don. I appreciate what you've done today. I know the rest of them do too." Don had never felt so proud of his mom as he did at that moment. "I'm going to see what I can do about getting some players tonight. Yes, sir. I'm betting we make it all the way to the playoffs this year."

When he walked away, Don remembered the conversation he'd had with his mom when he'd come home from school complaining about the math he knew he wasn't going to ever use again. Mom had sat down beside him and given him two bowls. She'd been making jelly all morning.

"All right. I have the instructions here on how to make jam. We're going to do something that has to do with the math you think you'll never use." He said it was dumb. "Perhaps, but you're going to take the ingredients and double them. That's what I need for me to be able to make the last of the blackberries into jam."

Don had the things he needed, but nothing to tell him the amounts. He figured since he liked it sweet, it should have a lot of sugar. And of course the berries. Mom asked him to add them last just in case he'd put too much into the bowl for them. Mom was doing the same thing he was, but she had the recipe to follow.

In the end, he'd failed. Not only had he failed, but in it, he'd ruined five pounds of sugar, the amount he'd guessed to go into the jam. Also, if he'd added the berries to his mess, he would have ruined two pints of his favorite kind of fruit. Mom's jam, of course, was perfect.

"Did you learn anything from this?" He told her he'd never be a jam maker. "You could, Don. You can do anything you set your mind to. However, today, for the rest of the day, I want you to think about every time you use math. You might have to concentrate on it, but by the end of the day, if you've not used math for something at least five times, you can get a tutor to help you out. If, and I'm thinking you'll see this, you do find five things, you'll work harder on what you don't perceive as something you'll use again."

He didn't even try all that hard to find things. When he'd been asked by one of his brothers to make some of the lemonade Mom always made for them in the summer, he'd used math to double it. Within the first hour after heading out the door to play with his brothers, Don had used math more times than he'd expected. It was something he used without even thinking about it. Calculating different ideas to make sure he had enough bricks to build something. To see if he had enough money to buy himself a slice of pizza at the party house.

Don told her he'd work harder. His mom never once told him she'd told him so. She never asked him what he'd figured out. But every night after that, she'd been there to help him if he had a question as to what he was doing in all subjects. Don, to this day, thought his mom was the smartest person he'd ever known.

At the end of practice, he gathered all the kids up. He told them about Robby and that he was home resting until Friday — two days on the couch with plenty to drink and eat. Don asked them if they'd go by and see him to make sure he was doing as he was told.

"Also, I want to tell you about the team. We, as I think you've noticed, do not have enough players to make a team. If you know anyone that wants to play this year, tell them to give me a call. As you know, there are rules in place that they must adhere to. No failing classes. No trouble with any of the teachers, as well as no medical conditions that will keep them from being able to play every game." One of the kids, he thought his name was Arnold, asked if everyone was going to play. "That's a good question. And I can tell you honestly, I have no idea. I want to have everyone out on the field for some of each game. However, that's not always possible. That is something we're going to have to deal with as we get going."

As he answered questions, paperwork was handed out to each player. He didn't mention anything that was there except to tell them they couldn't play without enough players. Don wanted to make sure that was something they knew right away.

After the players left, he picked up things off the field that had been scattered. Water bottles that had been left behind were put in the locker room to be claimed tomorrow. Also, he made sure there were enough drinks in the cooler to give the kids if they didn't have enough for their practice. Don was just turning to leave the big room when he noticed he wasn't alone anymore.

"May I help you?" The man nodded, but still didn't say anything. Getting a little nervous, he asked the man again if he needed anything. "I'm just heading out now. If you need something, let me know."

"I wanna help you." Nodding, he reached out to the man and realized he was handicapped. "I can't play no more, but I wanna help play. Momma said I could ask you if you were here by yourself. The other kids, they might fun at me."

"I won't allow that. What's your name?" He told him his name was Benson. "All right, Benson, let me get you some paperwork, and you'll have your momma fill it out for you. You'll also have to have a doctor check you over to make sure you're not going to be in any pain while we're playing."

"I got all that right here. Mr. Duncan, he's my helper, he gave it to me yesterday." Nodding, he took the paperwork from the man. "I'm not right in the head. I'm not supposed to call me retarded, but the kids do it all the time."

"I won't allow anyone to make fun of you, Benson. If they do, they won't play either." Benson grinned at him. "Okay, I'll need to talk to your momma too. Is she here?"

"Yes. Mr. Mason, he's my neighbor, he telled my

momma that you were a good man and that you might need me to help out." Don told him he could always use help. "I won't hurt nobody, Mr. Don. I'm addled, but I'm not mean. I promise you with all my body that I'd never hurt nobody."

"I believe you." He looked over the paperwork, then found the note attached to the back of his medical record. He read it and felt his heart tighten up when he realized this man was going to need this team more than he did anything in his life. "All right, Benson. You go on out and bring your momma here, and I'll give her the practice schedule. Also, I'll get you a shirt to wear that says you're a coach. All right?"

It took Don an hour to get things squared away with Rhonda Giles. She thanked him so many times he wanted to just tell her to stop. It wasn't anything for him to hire her son to help them.

"As I said in the letter, he doesn't have a great deal of companionship with anyone but me. He's been my protector since he was born. I never tried to overprotect him when he was growing up, so he isn't very tender about people making fun of him. I don't have long to live, Don. I want him to be able to function at things like helping someone, so he's not completely dependent on people to care for him." Don asked her what had happened. "To me or my son? Benson was born with the cord around his neck. The doctors didn't want to save him, but I made them. He'd been strangled for too long, they told me. I didn't care. He's the best part of me. I have cancer that wasn't caught early enough for me to survive it. "

"I'm sorry." She shrugged as she turned from him. Don could see she was really fighting with her grief. "I can go by your home and pick Benson up in the morning if you'd like. It's not far from where I live. That way, I can make sure he's got everything he needs."

"I have the list. Roger handed it off to me when he left here today. I know I should have waited until tomorrow, but once Benson found out there was a new coach here, he was too excited to wait. The other coach, he made fun of him for wanting to help out with the team. I think Benson would just be happy to fill up water bottles for the kids." Don told her he had a few jobs he thought Benson could help him out with. "Whatever you want him to do. The only thing I ask is that you don't hurt him. Physically or mentally. Please? As I said, he's all I have right now."

"I'd never hurt him. I'd rather cut off my right arm than harm him or anyone else. I promise you, if the kids so much as tease him, I'll cut them from the team." She told him that would make Benson a target. "Yes, I suppose you'd know. But he won't be hurt here. I want you to know that from the start. If it becomes a problem, which I don't foresee it happening, then I'll talk to you about it."

Don finished up what he'd been doing when Benson

and his mom left. There were a few things he thought Benson could do for him and the team. He decided right then and there that he was going to make sure not only that Benson had a good experience working with him, he would also be a part of the team when it came to being out front when pictures were taken, as well as when they were listed in the team books.

I was just wondering something. He smiled when Parker spoke to him. *This is really something I've only just started thinking about. But how would you feel if I suggested that the two of us meet at the hospital nursery? Your grandma has set this thing up for us. Or I'm not sure, but she could be setting us up. I wasn't sure what her deal was until I got a call from the hospital nursery, telling me that my appointment was confirmed to come and see the baby.*

Did you ask her after you got the call if she was setting us up? Parker told him she'd gone out of town for the day, and she wasn't going to be able to be reached. *She doesn't want us to yell at her, I'm thinking. Not that I would, but this is sounding a great deal like we're being told to have a baby soon. Perhaps sooner.*

I got more details than she gave me. It's a baby boy. He's not human, but the two women working today couldn't find in the notes what he was. I told her I'd be able to tell. Okay, so, his mother gave him up. She wants nothing to do with the child and was only there to deliver him then leave. She asked him if he could do something like that. Before he could answer, she continued. *He's physically fine. Mentally, of course, they* can't tell right now. But he's a bruiser. Weighed in at nearly ten pounds at birth.

That is a big fella. I'm headed there now. She said she was in the lobby waiting for him. *What would you have done if I said no?*

Seen him anyway, then beat the ever loving shit out of you when I got home. By the way, I've not told anyone else about this. Grandma said she'd not either. Also, my grandda is with me. He needed to pick up a couple of things in town. Tomorrow he's headed back to his house. I guess he's decided to sell it and move closer to us. Don asked her if he was going to come back to live with them. *He said he is but wants to square away the house first.*

Don pulled up in front of the hospital just as Parker was coming out with her grandda. They were both laughing, and he wondered what was going on. Not that it mattered. He loved the elderly man very much. He'd become the father he'd never had, it seemed like.

~~~

Peter tried very hard not to see any of the babies in the nursery. He'd been sitting out in the waiting room for over ten minutes now, and he just couldn't stand it any longer. There was a baby in there that might need him.

Going to stand outside the nursery windows, he saw the baby boy right away. Good heavens, he looked like he was six months old. He had fat cheeks, and so much hair on his head Peter was jealous. When he yawned, crunching up his little face, Peter wanted to grab him up and take him home with him. He turned, tearing his eyes away from the kid when Parker called to him.

"You have to come in here. They're going to bring him to us to hold, and you have the most experience of any of us." He said he'd only held Peter when he was a baby, and that had been a long time ago. "Well, that's more than Don or I either one have held, dolls or kids. Get in here with us or so help me, I'm going to make you walk home."

She wouldn't, and they both knew it. But Peter did go into the little room and wash up as he'd been told. As soon as they brought the little boy into the room, he nearly knocked Don down to be the first one to touch him. *Christ almighty*, he thought, *this could be my very first grandson.*

He was as heavy as he looked. When he opened his little eyes, Peter had to hold back on the tears. Peter wasn't aware you could fall in love with someone at first sight, but he had. The little man had not only captured his heart, but he was pretty sure he'd do just about anything for him. Now or in the future.

"Are you going to show us what to do?" He looked at Parker and pretended to hide the baby away. "I'm terrified."

"Good heavens, girl, there is nothing to be afraid of. Come on, sit here, and I'll show you what you have to do." It was hard for him to hand him over, but he was glad he was able to pass him on to Parker. "Make sure you keep his neck held so that his head doesn't flop around. Also, be careful of his head. He has some kind of soft spot up there, I guess."

"You guess?" He laughed with Don. "He might be a big kid to most, but to me, he's a tiny little thing. I mean, he fits in my hand."

"Yes, well, no one is going to be toting him around with just one hand on him, or I'll step in." Peter felt a little ashamed of himself for saying that. But both of his grandkids—he'd already adopted Don as his own—told him it was fine. "You're not going to leave him here, are you? I mean, if they'd let me, I'd take him home with me. But I'm sure they have rules about sixty-something-year-old men adopting children."

But that was just what he wanted. He was having a good time getting to know all the other people in the family, taking their time with all the things going on. He loved everything about them. However, he was sure if he tried to run out of here with an infant in his hands, they'd tell him to hit the road. As he watched Parker and Don with the child, he thought this was the best thing for not just the child, but him as well. They would be the perfect parents for any child, he thought.

It took them an hour to get things squared away with Peter Donahue Foster. He not only loved the name but was proud of the fact that he'd been named for him. Also, Peter was very glad to find out that the child wasn't human but was a lion cub. Parker said it would make things easier for him to be with people the same as he was. Peter believed her, knowing the things that would have befallen him if he'd been adopted to a human family. It would have been difficult for the child.

They were given a car seat for the baby to come home in, along with formula and diapers. That was an area none of them were knowledgeable on. The kind nurses made sure they knew what sort of things they'd need when they got home. Most of the things on the market, she'd told him, were just put out for the furniture companies. Peter had no trouble believing that.

Surprised to be having dinner with the three of them, he thought he should have given them this time alone. But Parker wouldn't hear of it, and Don was happy to have him along. People from all over the restaurant came to look at little Pete. Calling him Pete seemed to be the consensus.

The baby slept through it all, and Peter was excited to get him back to the house so he could hold him again. It was the hardest thing he'd ever done to wait on someone to give him permission to hold his very first great-grandchild again. He looked at Don when he started to laugh.

"You do know that as his grandparent, especially his great grandda, you can pretty much get away with all kinds of things. If you want to hold him, Peter, just pick him up. I don't think it will hurt him or you at all if he got some extra loving today. He's been abandoned

and adopted in just the first couple of days of his life."
Reaching in the car seat for Pete, he was happy when he
looked at him. "In a few days, less I'm betting, you won't
have a chance to hold him anytime you want. Remember,
he has a grandma and great-grandma that will want to
take him from you too."

"We'll just have to see about that, won't we, little
man?" Holding him was like having sunshine in his
arms. All the warmth of happiness that he could want.
Mostly, he loved holding him because he was his. His
great-grandson. His little man. Peter was going to teach
him everything he knew. "I'm going to tell you all about
your grandda—my little boy. You and I will have such
adventures together, I'm thinking. We'll be like two peas
in a pod."

Peter did find himself being depressed about his
wife, however. She'd been so depressed after Peter was
murdered. He had too. Peter wondered if he had paid a
little more attention to her back then whether she might
have been here to enjoy this little man. It was something
that would haunt him at times.

"I just thought of something I'd like the two of you to
do. You should name your children anything you wish,
but I was thinking if you had yourself a little girl, my late
wife and my mom would be perfect names—also your
mother, Don. My mom's name was Elizabeth Marie. My
father's name, of course, was Peter. Dad called Mom Em
when they were both alive. I think with all the family you

guys have, it would be simple to figure out a name for a child easily. I just wanted to put my two cents in there." He looked at Parker, wanting to let her know how she made him feel by making him a part of all this. "I never thought, not in all my life, that I'd ever be able to hold a grandbaby in my arms. This feels wonderful. I wanted you to know that this little man and any children you have, they're going to be my everything."

He wasn't going to die. Peter had been told that yesterday when he and Don had sat down in the living room to talk. Mae had been buried that morning, and he'd been feeling sorry for Raymond. The pain of loss was something Peter had known all too well in his life.

Don smacked him upside the head and then laughed. "I've been calling for you for the last ten minutes. Where were you?" He said that he'd been thinking of all the people he'd lost. "I know what you're going through. My dad was a prick and a bastard. He beat us and our mom. But let me ask you what my grandma asked me. Can you change anything? Could you have loved your wife any more or less? Is there a way that you could change anything by feeling sorry for yourself?"

"No. I mean, I don't know that I could." Don asked him if he thought he might have. "I don't think it would have mattered to my wife at all what I did. She was in a deep depression for so long after Peter was murdered."

"Good. Then you have to let it go. If you don't, it's going to eat you alive. Since you're an immortal now, that is going to be a very long time for you to have something eating away at you that you could no more change than you could the fact that she's gone. Right?" He nodded. "Tell me something, Peter. If I could make it happen for you, what if you were to become a part of the high school where I teach? I've recently found out that you have a doctorate in social justice. Also, that you're an attorney. They could use someone in human resources with your kind of skills."

"I think I'd like that." Don nodded and smiled at him. "Is this your way of telling me I've been lazing round the house long enough?"

"Sort of. But I've figured out that having something to do makes the days go by better. I like being with people. I'm sure you do as well." He said he missed that by living alone. "You need to get out and be human again. Be a man about town. You need to be a person anyone would feel comfortable coming to when they have issues. Kids would love to have you around at the school."

"I think I might enjoy steering kids in the right direction too." The more they talked about it, the more excited he became. So now he was going to start school in August, being the head of the HR department of the local high school. "Thank you for that, Don. You hit the nail right on the head with this."

"It was my pleasure. You're a good man, Peter. I'm glad to have you as part of this family."

He was so touched by his words that he hugged the

younger man. And when he wrapped his arms around him, Peter, still to this day, felt he could take on the world and win.

As soon as they pulled into the drive of their home, he was given the pleasure of carrying Pete into the house. He was so excited to have the first picture with him too that he was hard-pressed to give him up to Meggie. But he did. And in that moment, a moment that he'd remember forever, he kissed Meggie on the cheek and told her how he was going to enjoy being a grandparent with her.

"That's right. We will be. I can't think of a nicer person to share that with than you." They both laughed and laughed again over the baby's head. Pete woke up then and fussed about being squashed. "We're grandparents, Peter. Do you believe it?"

"I do, and I'm so glad I have you to thank for this." He kissed her again. "I'm already head over heels in love with this family. And this little guy makes is even better."

Chapter 10

Benson was afraid now that he was here on the ball field. After being introduced to the team, he hung back so he'd not get in the way. Mr. Don told him his job was to make sure he kept an eye on all the players, to make sure they rested when they were looking exhausted and that they had plenty of water. It wasn't until the first kid he'd been watching limped to the starting line that he realized it wasn't a lame job, but a most important one.

"You need to get off the team." The kid just looked at him. That was when Benson noticed his eyes were all wrong. "You can't play here. You have to go home. No drugs. No drugs."

"Says who? You? I don't listen to retards." It hurt him terribly to have someone say that to him. But his momma had told him to stand up for himself because he was the only one that could sometimes. "Get out of my way, retard. My dad will eat you alive if you fuck with me."

Pulling his whistle out of his shirt, Benson blew on it as hard as he could. All the coaches had one. It was an emergency thing, Mr. Don told him. All the coaches came running to him when he put his whistle back under his shirt. The kid, he didn't know his name, started complaining about him right away.

"He's trying to be bossy to me, Coach. He thinks he's in charge or something. I don't want him near me when I'm trying to practice with my team." Mr. Don asked Benson what he found. "Nothing. This person hasn't anything—"

"He's not right." Mr. Mason asked him what he meant. "I don't know the words, but he's not right. You have to look at his eyes and his arms. He's not right. No drugs. The sign says no drugs."

Mr. Don was the one that understood first. Pulling the kid toward him, he jerked his sleeve up and looked at his arm. It was all marked up with holes. The bruising on it looked like his momma's arms did when she went in for her treatment.

"Roger, call the police, please." The kid started screaming at them that it was nothing more than a cut he'd gotten. That his dad had money, and they were going to regret treating him like this. Mr. Don wasn't having it. "Call them and tell them that Larry Jude is high as a kite and that he's getting it from his parents."

By the time the police got there, Benson was as scared

as he'd ever been. Larry was still yelling at him, calling him names. The other kids were standing around too. Mr. Don looked at him and asked him if he was all right.

"I'm not a retard." Mr. Don told him he certainly wasn't. "He called me that. I don't like it. But he's been doping up, and that's not right either. I don't want to lose my job, Mr. Don."

"You aren't going to, Benson. Without you, I wouldn't have seen this. This is why I needed you to keep an eye on the kids. Not just this, but in the event one of them gets sick. It's an important duty, and I'm so glad you did the right thing."

Benson nodded but wasn't so sure. The other kids were looking at him funny too. Backing away from it all, Robby, a nice boy, asked him if he was all right. Nodding, Robby shook his head before speaking again.

"You're not all right. You're upset. I would have been too if he called me names. Don't be. Some of us knew he was high, but we're afraid of him." Benson asked him why. "Well, the biggest reason is his parents are meaner than snot. Also, he has money. Enough to hurt us if we were to have told on him. I'm glad you did it, Benson. You did the perfect thing with this. Thanks."

It was still hard for him to get it into his head that he wasn't going to be in trouble. The police asked him questions about how he'd known. After telling them about Larry's eyes and stuff, the officer shook his hand. It was the best thing he'd had happen to him in all his life.

"Can you show us how to do the pick-up and run drill, Benson? It's a lot harder than I thought. If you can show us like you did first thing this morning, we might get it better." Robby was pulling him away from the ambulance that was checking out Larry. "I think some of us got it, but I don't understand how we're to make it work with eleven guys from the other team running at us."

Benson enjoyed working one on one with the boys. Whenever he'd look in the direction of the police and medical team, someone would get him back to helping. He wanted to be good at his job and not mess up any. He really hoped Mr. Don didn't fire him.

Benson watched football all the time at home in the cool weather. He had some moves he'd picked up from there that kept him busy with the boys. By the time Larry was taken away, he had them running drills with the dummies. The kind that they had to hit, not ones like him.

When practice was over, Mr. Don called him and the other coaches in to have a meeting with the players. He was ever so glad that it was in the building. He was sweating like a hog on a hot summer day. As soon as they were all given something to drink, Mr. Don started out by telling them to applaud him. Benson didn't know what to think when the boys not only clapped for him but thanked him a lot for getting Larry away from them.

"Benson took a big chance today in calling out Larry.

That is the reason I've hired him to work with us. Also, I noticed he was working well with the rest of you, keeping you working even though there was other stuff going on. You're a team, and I'm thrilled to death to see that you can work well under all kinds of situations." Mr. Don shook his hand too. "You did a good solid for all of us today, Benson. I can't thank you enough for it."

When his momma came to pick him up after he was done helping clean up, he was almost too excited to tell her what happened. But he shouldn't have worried about it. Mr. Don and the rest of the staff told her about it and made it seem like he'd saved the day. Even the team, before they left, was talking to his mom and making sure she knew he'd been there for them all.

As soon as he got home, he had to sit in his room with the lights off. He was too excited. When he got that way, he would mess up. The last time he'd been this excited, he'd wet his pants. Benson rocked back and forth in his special corner until he could think with his mind again.

"You did a good job today at your work. I'm very proud of you, Benson." He kissed her on the cheek and told her he had so much fun. "I'm happy for you. I knew Mr. Don wouldn't steer you wrong."

Benson fixed his momma and him a salad for dinner. She said she was just too exhausted to eat, but he did get her to take a few bites. After she went to bed, he washed up the dishes and put things away. Checking on her before he went to bed, it scared him a bit when she started coughing and couldn't stop. Benson put the phone down when she laid back on her bed. He was ready to call the doctor if she got any sicker.

"I want to tell you something. You're not going to like it, but I have to tell you, all right?" He nodded, then asked her if she was going to die soon. "I am. Very soon. I can't hang on much longer, Benson. I'm hurting badly all the time now, and it's just too much on me. I don't want to leave you, but I'm afraid I will."

"I don't want you to hurt no more, Momma. I know you do all the time, too." She said she did and started coughing again. Benson picked up the phone, but she asked him to put it back on the cradle for now. "I want to call you some help when you need it, Momma. You showed me how."

"I did, but there won't be a thing they can do to help me." Benson started to cry when Momma asked him to listen to her. "If you find me when I've passed on, you call the ambulance first thing. I'll be gone, so they'll know what to do for me. Then I want you to call Mrs. Parker, Mr. Don's wife. Her phone number is right there by the phone for you. She came by today and helped me with a few arrangements. The doctor told me it's only a matter of time now."

Benson wasn't sure what that meant, but he nodded anyway. It was wearing his momma out talking to him, but he was careful not to get too upset about what she was telling him. The only thing he had to worry about, she told him, was that he didn't get upset with anyone, and maybe they'd let him live in this house alone.

When she closed her eyes, he sat with her for a while. Watching every breath she did, in and out, Benson could tell how hard it was for her. Also, Benson could tell she wasn't breathing the way she should have been. Picking up the phone, he went to the kitchen to get the number for Mrs. Parker.

"Mrs. Parker, this is Benson. My momma said I should call you after the ambulance was called. My momma, she's not breathing too good." Mrs. Parker said she'd be right there. "I don't want her to die. She's all I got in the whole wide world." He couldn't help but cry then. His heart was broken. Mrs. Parker didn't make fun of him at all. She just kept saying it was all right that he called her.

"You stay with your momma, Benson, and I'll be right there with my husband. Would you like me to bring anyone else with me? We've all been told that your momma is really sick." Benson said he'd be all right with Mr. Don too. "All right. We'll be there in a few minutes. You just stay with your momma and hold her hand. She'll know you're right there with her."

When he hung up the phone, he laid down beside his momma. Taking her hand into his, he held it gently, not wanting to hurt her anymore. He told her about his day and how much he had fun. Benson also told her how much he loved her.

Counting as high as he could, up to fifty, he would

count off numbers when his mom would breathe in, then out. She was all the way up to thirty-five now between her breathing, and it worried him something terrible.

"Momma, you're my best friend in the whole wide world. I know you're hurting, and I'm sorrier than I ever been about it. If you need to stop breathing, I want you to know I'll be all right." He knew he'd not be. Benson had never been alone in his life. But he knew his momma was hurting bad. "I love you, Momma. I love you to the moon and back."

The number got all the way to fifty this time, then to five again when he counted. It was getting harder and harder to count them on account of her breathing so soft. When the door opened and closed in the living room, he didn't even get up. Mrs. Parker was coming into the room with Mr. Don.

"She's not breathing good." Mrs. Parker told him she was sorry. "I don't know what to do. I told her if she needed to stop breathing, it would be all right. I'd be all right. But I don't know that I can be. I got nobody else."

"You have us, Benson." Mr. Don hugged him tightly as soon as Benson stood up. "You'll always have us. My entire family is going to be here for you. We'll not let you be alone."

The next time he counted his momma's breaths, he got to fifty-three times before he realized she wasn't going to breathe again. Holding her hand in his, he rocked back and forth, crying hard about how much he loved her. His momma had been good to him, and now she was gone. Mr. Don, he said he'd take care of making the phone calls. Benson never left his momma's side as she passed on to Heaven.

The police came in first. They were ever so nice to him, telling him he could say his goodbyes to her, and they'd not bother him. The man with the big old ambulance came too, and he waited in the other room. Mrs. Parker, she was nice too.

After his momma was taken away, he sat on the bed, rocking and crying. Mr. Don told him there were things for him to do. Things that the funeral director needed from him. Mrs. Parker helped him pick out his momma's favorite dress then. He'd been scared by how it wasn't going to fit her. Momma had been a big woman, but she was nothing but twigs now.

"It's fine, Benson. They'll make it fit." He asked her if they had someone there to sew it in for her. "I think they'll figure it out. Don't you? Now, did your momma have some shoes that she wore with this dress? Perhaps a hat. I noticed she had quite a collection of them."

"Momma liked hats; she sure did. After she'd get her treatments, she'd wear one of them when she had to go out to the grocery. I think it was like a party when she wore them." Benson picked out the blue one she'd worn the last time he'd seen her wearing a hat. "I don't want her to be looking like she's sleeping, Mrs. Parker. Do you think there is something we can tell the funeral man, so she looks like she's been out having fun? I sure would like that."

"I'll do that for you. I think you're correct too. She would have loved that idea, Benson." They looked through her dresses again and found one that looked bright and fun. He'd not seen her wear it in a long time and was happy to see there was a pretty hat to go with it. "Now, we need to see what you can wear. Don and I have talked it over, and we want you to come and stay with us for a few days. At least until the funeral is over. That way, you won't have to worry about answering questions you might not know the answer too."

"Oh, no. I can't be pushing into your house." He didn't think he'd said that right, but she told him it would be nice for them to have him there. Then she told him about the new baby. "You got yourself a baby? Oh my lordy, I bet he's a cute little man."

"He's not so little. With you there, you can hold him too. He loves people." Benson told her he wasn't to hold babies. "You can hold my baby, Benson. I'd be very happy to allow you to do that. You might even help me out by feeding him a bottle or two while you're staying there."

Benson was worried these people didn't understand he wasn't right in the head. The more she talked about him helping her out with little Pete, the more he realized she didn't care what was wrong with him. Benson, she told him, was a part of her family now, and he could be

Pete's honorary uncle.

"I've never been an uncle to nobody before." She said he'd be a special uncle for him too. An honorary one. "I don't know what that means, but I'll be the best honorary one he ever had."

By the time they got to Mr. Don's house, he was exhausted. His body was hurting from working. And he'd not had a wink of sleep in all the time he'd been home yesterday.

Every time he thought about home, he'd hurt for his momma. She was in Heaven now, not hurting at all. Mr. Don found him a place to lay down. Benson wanted to hold the little boy, but he knew he needed to rest. If he got too tired, he might hurt the little boy. This was better. Almost as soon as he laid his head down on the softest pillow he'd ever felt, his body just fell asleep before his head did.

~~~

Shirley walked around the house twice before she settled back in the dining room. Anna was already there, playing with her new toys. This house was better than anything she'd ever lived in, along with the fact that she had a good job and a place to hide from David. She wondered what he had been thinking beating up on one of the Foster men.

"Mom, I was thinking about something." Shirley sat down at the new dining room table and ran her hand along the smooth surface while asking Anna what she'd been thinking about. "You got a nice job now. And I heard Ms. Parker saying you have insurance for all kinds of stuff. Does that mean we can go to the eye doctor too?"

"Yes." She watched her daughter as she played with the crafting kit she'd been given. "Are you thinking you need glasses or something? The last time you were checked out, they said you were seeing just fine."

"I was thinking about you." It had never entered her mind that she could use the insurance too. All her life since her daughter had been born, she'd been making everything about her. Doctors, food, and the things that would keep her safe. "I see you reading on the tablet thingy you got, and I think you need to go and get checked out soon."

She could, she realized. Ms. Parker had given her an advance on her first check so that she and Anna could go to the store. However, once they were there, it seemed like every Foster in the state had shown up to help her. By the time they were finished up and loading things into the two trucks that were there, they had enough food in the house for an army, she thought.

"They're very generous, aren't they? I mean, I thought they were nice when I kept hearing about how they were helping out people in the town. But to know that all of them are about as nice as the other one, it's surprising, I guess." Anna told her about meeting Grandma Jane. "Yes, she was at the grocery with us. Remember?"

"I do. She made you buy both kinds of ice cream

instead of just what I like." Anna was putting away her things when she looked at her again. "They paid for this house too, didn't they, Mom? And the food and stuff we're using."

"Yes. We owe them a great debt. I'm not allowed to repay them because they said we need to pass on the help that we got. But to consider it a loan on happiness." Anna hugged her tightly. "This right here could be a wonderful thing to pay people back with. You, my dear child, give the best hugs ever."

The closer it got to dinner, the more she wanted to go out and try the new grill. She'd never done anything like it before, had a grill that worked every time you wanted to cook on it. And there was no charcoal to wait on either. Just turn it on and then wait for it to warm up to cook. Shirley asked Anna what she wanted to cook out.

"Oh, Mom. When I was at the Foster house, they had salmon on the grill. It looked so good, and it was as tender as a slice of bread." She said she didn't know anything about cooking fish on the grill. "Me either, but I was thinking the next time we went there, we could ask them. But I'd love a burger hot off the grill. And some grilled onions. Remember that place we went to, and that's what they had?"

She did remember that. It was the only time they'd been out to eat. The place had only just opened up, and they were giving away free treat burgers. Asking Anna to see if she could find a recipe on how to do that, she said she'd give it a try.

They had fun looking up things to try and cook. As it turned out, they had several things going on the grill at one time. Burgers, of course, but they also tried grilled onions, carrots, as well as mushrooms. Anna had found a tray of chicken strips too, and she put them on. Their plan was to use them on a salad this week.

Sitting at the table when they were finished, the two of them ate off the large platters she'd used and took bites of all of the things they'd cooked. They were still keeping track of their favorites when someone rang the front doorbell.

Shirley was halfway there when she remembered what Parker had told her—never answer a door straight on. Always come to it from the side. While she understood the reasoning behind it, she had been worried that Parker had seemed so forceful about her remembering that. Just as she slid to the side of the door, the entire door exploded inward, throwing pieces of wood all the way back to the kitchen.

Yelling at Anna to run, she was happy when she made her way to the back of the house and into the area where the walk-in freezer was. There was a secondary door back there that only unlocked from the inside. Her daughter was safe. That was a wonderful feeling to her. Shirley realized she'd been hit when standing up after the blast was hard.

Where are you? Not even thinking about how she was

speaking to Parker, she told her what had happened. *I'm on my way. Don't get killed by being stupid. You understand me?*

Yes. I'm rarely stupid just so you know. Having no idea why she was talking like nothing was going on, Shirley told her it was David. He had a gun. *I'm in the dining room under the table. Anna is in the freezer. She might have gone out the back, but I can't tell from here. I'm hurt.*

She saw the woman she'd grown to admire in just a few days as she entered the room behind David. Shirley didn't speak, even when David was screaming for her. Instead, she closed her eyes and tried to calm her breathing. It was that or sob like a child. David was out for blood, and he wasn't going to be happy until she spilled out all of hers.

"Hello, David." David asked Parker where his wife was. "Your wife? You don't have a wife anymore. You were divorced. A couple of years ago, as a matter of fact. Did you know you're not supposed to be carrying a gun? Nor are you supposed to use it to get into a house that doesn't belong to you."

"Shut the fuck up. You've caused me enough shit." Parker asked him how she'd done that, she didn't even know him all that well. "Your family. They're all a bunch of pricks, did you know that?"

"No. The police are coming. If they weren't, I'd have had you dead by now. You're not worth me having to fill out a bunch of paperwork to kill you before they get here." David snarled something at Parker, but Shirley couldn't hear what it was. "You're such a mother fucker. I wanted to tell you that before you're picked up again. By the way, did you have some fun with my brother-in-law the other day? I heard it was quite a sight to see you being nicked around your small twig and berries. Loman told me it was hardly worth the effort to cut them."

"You shut the fuck up. You don't know shit." Looking down at her hand, Shirley wondered if she was going to die right here. "Where is Shirley and that brat of hers? They should be back at my house waiting on me, not out here living it up."

"Perhaps they'd be there, waiting on you, if you'd allowed them to live it up once in a while. But when you beat the shit out of someone on a daily basis, then things get a little out of control." Parker tisked at David. "You shot Shirley, David. While she won't die, there is a good possibility that you'll get a longer prison sentence for firing a weapon at her."

Shirley almost laughed. Just hearing Parker tell David she wasn't going to die made her feel so much better. Careful to not make any noises, she looked into the kitchen when someone made a sound. There stood Don. He was grinning from ear to ear too.

Go with Don, please. He's going to make sure you and Anna are safe. Nodding, she moved toward the man when Parker told her to go. *The police are pulling in now. You just —*

When her words were cut off, Shirley had just taken a step toward Don. Turning when the gun went off again, she watched in horror as Don went from a smiling man to a big lion in no time at all. Don, as a large lion, darted by her and out to the main hall where his wife and David were. Going to the freezer room, she saw that Anna wasn't in the large walk-in and went out the door. There on the grass was Anna and Mrs. Foster, Don's mom.

"Come along now. We're to head to the barn back here and await the others. I'm sorry, I can't tell you anything. The only thing I was asked to do was to come for you." Carmilla asked if she was all right. "That doesn't look too bad, my dear. I don't know if you were told this or not, but as a part of this family, you can't be killed by a mere bullet. I don't know what it would take, but I've been told to assure you you're going to be fine."

"It looks like it's not bleeding as much." Carmilla looked it over and declared it healed. Anna looked too and was so relieved to see that it was indeed healed, she hugged her tightly. Shirley asked if David was going to prison.

"That I can tell you, though I don't know how you're going to feel about it. I believe he's been shot but is going to heal. Parker said she could have killed him but didn't. She wants him to spend a lot of time in prison—nasty person. My husband was like that. True to her word, Brook saved me." Shirley told Carmilla how much she admired her daughters-in-law. "I do, as well. They're brilliant and funny. They scare me some too, but I'm almost over that."

The police joined them in the barn a few minutes later. David had been shot, but he'd done it himself while trying to aim his gun at Parker. Shirley wasn't sure why, but she believed Parker had hurt him, and the police, happy to have him out of the way, would agree to anything she said. Shirley loved the other woman and wished they'd met under different circumstances. She would love to have been a friend of hers.

You are my friend. Startled when Parker spoke to her, she moved from the police who were asking questions of Carmilla. *You're a good friend, and I'm glad we were able to help you out. I don't have a lot of female friends. They're intimidated by me. Not that I understand that.*

I do. You're this all powerful witch that has all sorts of freaky magic, and you don't have any trouble calling it like it is. They both laughed. *I can't thank you enough for all you've done for my daughter and me. We were having such fun before David came into the house.*

And you will again. I promise you. Now that he's broken all kinds of laws, they'll hold him until he goes to court. There is a long prison term for trying to shoot an officer of the law. It just so happens that the police department hired me as a consultant just today. Parker winked at her when she laughed. *But seriously, things will start to look up for both of you. Anna and my grandmother-in-law are practically joined at the hip now, they're such good friends.*

Once David was taken away by ambulance and the house put back in order, Don went to the hardware store to get them a new front door. This time, he told her he was going to make sure she had a camera on the door so she could see who was out there. They were about the nicest people in the world to have on your side.

After everyone left the house and her home was back in order, she and Anna sat on the couch to watch some television. She loved this little girl with all her heart and was glad she was so well adjusted. It couldn't have been easy living with David all the time and seeing him beat up on her. Shirley thought the first step was the hardest. And they were supposed to be easier as a person stepped away from whatever they were trying to get out of. They were finally beginning to feel like they were finally someplace they needed to be.

"I'm going to help other people when I get older. I want to be able to make sure people are safe. Like the Fosters did for us." Shirley told her that it was a great thing to strive to be. "Yes, I'm going to save up all the money I ever make so I can help people get a fresh start. Like Parker and Don did for me and you. We couldn't have done it without them, could we have?"

"No, we would still be running. Still be looking for someplace to be safe, live, and try to be like everyone else." Shirley kissed her daughter on the top of her head. "Anna, I love you. I couldn't be more proud of you than if you were president of the United States."

"Maybe I'll do that too. I think I'd make a good one. I'll start working on my acceptance speech now."

Shirley was still laughing as she went to bed later that night. It wouldn't surprise her to see her daughter in the White House either, she thought with a laugh.

Chapter 11

Glancing at the clock, Lily counted down the time she had left to work. Her feet hurt, her back was killing her, and she thought if she were to sit down right now, she'd never get up again. This was the problem with being overeducated, unmarried, with four kids at home wondering where their next meal was coming from. Smiling, she thought of her sister and what she was going to say to her when she arrived tomorrow night.

Lily knew the first thing she was going to say to her. She'd want to know where the hell her head had been when she'd taken on three kids that weren't hers. Lily would tell her what she said to anyone that asked. She loved them.

But she also knew Rogue would love them too. If nothing else, her sister would strive to be the best aunt to them and would love them as much as she did. Her sister was one of a kind.

A year and a half ago, Lily had been happy, about to be married and living in a home for the first time in her adult life. Then, as life would do sometimes, it shit on her. Mark was killed in a car accident. She assumed, sadly so, that she and the kids would be taken care of. But that didn't pan out either.

His ex-wife had sued her for the house and insurance before Mark had even been buried. Not only did she win the suit against her—even though everything, from the insurance and house to the cars in the garage, were in her name with Mark's—in the end, Lily had been left with nothing. Less than nothing, because while she'd been earning a nice check each week, the money had been in the checking account she'd shared with Mark. The bitch had gotten her money too.

The kids, however, had been nothing Missy, his ex-wife, had wanted. They were hers, of course, but since Mark had won full custody of them, she saw no reason to take them with her when she robbed them of even a home to live in. The attorney for Missy had told Lily several times how sorry he was, and that he wished he'd been on her side. Lily was glad she was there for them when their father had loved them so dearly. Even her own son, Gabe, Mark had treated the same as he had his own children.

"Lily, there's a phone call for you. I think it's your daughter." Nodding, she took the call in the boss's office of the restaurant she worked in. Billy, at fifteen, was in charge of the others when she had to work.

"Mom, there is a person here who says she's your sister. She's nothing like you, is she? If she is your sister. I don't know if I like her or not." Lily laughed and asked her to put her on the phone. "I'd have to let her in. Are you willing to bet she's your sister?"

"All right. To test your theory, and it is a good one, ask her what her first name is. If she won't tell you, it's her. By the way, her middle name is Rogue. She won't allow anyone to call her by her first one." She heard Billy asking her what her first name was, and the reply she got from Rogue.

"You tell your mother that I'm going to kick her ass all the way to my car and back if she so much as gives anyone my fucking first initial. You tell her I didn't come all this way to—" Billy must have believed her because she was talking to Rogue as she finished talking about the things she was going to do to her when she found her. "I'm not above kicking your ass, even though you're older than me."

"I believe you. I'm so glad you're there. But I thought you weren't coming until tomorrow. What happened?" Rogue didn't answer her but asked a question of her own. "Yes, we're staying in a one bedroom apartment. It's all I can afford. There is plenty of room if you discount the fact that I'm rarely home anymore, trying to keep up with the rent and food for the five of us."

"One of them is giving me the evil eye right now.

Doesn't she know I'm her aunt, and the one she should be buttering up?" Lily told Rogue they didn't understand buttering people up, as they didn't know anyone with anything they would share with them. "You need to get you a good attorney, Lily. If I had been around, she never would have gotten away with this."

"Yes, well, that costs money. Money I don't have. I'm so glad you're here. I've missed you. Where are you going to stay?" She asked her if she could move them in with her. "I don't know, Rogue. Are you still living out of a suitcase?"

"Pretty much. But today I'm in a hotel that has three rooms and a kitchenette. I'm going to gather the kids up, hit a pizza place, and meet you after work." She told her the name of the hotel she was staying at. "If you want, I can come pick you up. The kid in charge here said you walked to work because you have no car. Didn't I tell you I'd pay for one for you to use until I could make it back here?"

"That would be Billy. She's fifteen." Rogue asked her how she could keep them all straight. "You can do that when you love them as much as I do. I'll be getting off here at around eleven. If you could pick me up, I'd love it. I'm too exhausted to walk much more today."

Lily knew that by the time she got home, not only would Rogue have all their names straight, but she'd know everything there was to know about them. She'd even bet they'd have a few changes of good clothing, a toy or two if they wanted, and Billy and Gabe, the oldest two, would have some kind of handheld game that Rogue knew how to play as well as any teenager.

At eleven, Lily clocked out. She'd done well in tips tonight and was still counting them out when her sister pulled up in a gray SUV. All four of her children were in the back seats and buckled in properly. Lily asked her what she was doing with such a big car.

"I rented it while I'm here. By the way, I was told none of them needed to be in a car seat. I'm still thinking smart mouth back there, Donna, needs to have a roll of tape over her mouth. She's just like me." With a large grin from Rogue, Lily turned to look at Donna. She gave her a thumbs up. "I'm moving you into a house I rented. I don't want to hear about how you're fine in that place you were at. There is only one bathroom and five people sharing it. You know me, can't stand to share anything."

"You're a wonderful sharer. Is that a word?"

Rogue pulled out of the parking lot and onto the road. It was on the tip of her tongue to ask her how far she was going to be walking now but didn't. The kids were talking quietly, the music, something that Rogue had on all the time, was just background noise, and the seat was comfy.

Being awakened by the door opening and the light coming on startled her. Turning in the seat to count the kids, something she did every time they were out, she saw they were pulling things from the back of the car.

Getting out, Rogue handed her a heavy bag of what appeared to be food and told her to take it in the house.

It was just after one in the morning when the kids finally made it up to the bedrooms. Lily just wanted to lie down and never wake up, but Rogue said she wanted to talk to her about something. Lily had seen how much she'd paid for the food before Rogue had snatched the receipt from her and wanted to say a few things to her as well.

"Okay. Two things. I can afford whatever is running through your mind to say to me about the purchases tonight. More if you need it. The house belongs to a buddy of mine who is out of the country right now. In effect, we're doing him a favor, he told me, by being here and keeping the lights on. Also, I have another friend that has a brother who is an attorney. I'm going to call him first thing in the morning. There is no reason whatsoever she should have gotten anything at all from Mark's estate." Lily felt her eyes fill with tears. "If you start crying, I'm going to cry, and we're going to be a slobbery mess when the kids get up in a few hours."

"I've so missed you." They hugged again. They'd been hugging since they got here, and it felt better every time they did. "Missy, the kids' mom, told the judge right there in the courtroom that the kids were heathens anyway, and should be with me. Rogue, the kids were in the room when she said that. How could anyone do that to a child, let alone their own child?"

"There are plenty of people out there that would, and who do it daily. She's shit, and we're going to take care of her as soon as possible." Lily told her she hoped so. "I know you've not done it yet, so I will. We need to call Dad and make him aware of what is going on. I know you and him parted on bad terms, but this isn't likely to get resolved soon, and it would be nice if he was in your corner."

"He was having an affair when Mom was laying there dying." Rogue didn't comment, but she knew what she was thinking. "It doesn't matter that Mom had been in a coma for eight years. He should have been faithful to her. Getting married not a month after she was laid to rest was a terrible thing to do to her memory."

"What sort of memories do you have of Mom, Lily? Want me to tell you about mine? She had a stroke when I was barely two. From that point on, the only time I saw her was when Dad would load us up in the car and take us to see her at the nursing home. I haven't any idea what her voice sounded like. I don't know the color of her eyes. She wasn't ever able to do any of the things for me that she did for you when you were younger. No cookie baking. No PTA meetings. Mom was in a coma when I needed her. How do you think Dad coped when he needed someone?" Lily told her it wasn't Mom's fault. "No, it wasn't anyone's fault. Mom had a stroke that took her away from both of us, but especially Dad. And he did try. You know that."

"I know. But only a month. I was just getting used to not going to see her when he married again." Rogue again said nothing. "I guess we're still going to agree to disagree about this."

"I suppose so. But I have something I'd like for you to think about. We had each other when Mom was alive. Dad had no one. Did he ever bring her to our home? Did Dad ever once mention to either of us that he was finding love someplace else? No, he didn't. You want to know why he might have done that? Because he never wanted us to be hurt. I think what he did in sparing us was more loving than anything anyone could have done for us." Lily hadn't thought of it that way. "Another thing he did too. He didn't ever not visit Mom every day. He took care of her the best he could when she came home from the nursing home in those last days. He did this, all by himself, while we got to live and have a life. Dad did all of that for us. Then after Mom passed, Dad got to live for himself. I think what he did took a great deal of courage. Things could have been a great deal different if he'd not loved and respected Mom the way he did."

When Rogue went to bed, Lily sat there for another hour. Everything Rogue said was true. Some of it was things she'd said to her before, but thinking back on the way they had lived while their mom was alive, Lily could see their dad trying hard to make their lives as normal as possible. Yes, he'd done that, and more, for both of them. Lily decided to give him a call tomorrow.

Lily got up at seven, nearly an hour after she should have been up and moving. The kids were going to be late for school. They didn't have their lunches made, and she was really thinking about letting them stay home for the day when she made it to the kitchen. The house was empty of any sound. The note on the table had her snatching it up, sure that someone had taken her children from her.

"Breathe and calm the hell down." She let out a long breath when she read the first words that her sister had written on the note. "I gave the kids lunch money and took them to school. Gabe has given me a list of things they'll need now, and I'm picking it up on the way home. If you're reading this, just sit down, calm down, and have whatever you drink in the morning, and I'll be there soon. Christ, I love these kids."

Lily was brewing a cup of tea that was on the counter when Rogue came back. Her usual brew was a cup of coffee, but there didn't seem to be a coffee maker in the room. Helping her bring in the things she'd picked up, Lily was positive that a computer wasn't on the list her son had given his aunt.

"It wasn't. I need it. If they can use it too, that's fine by me. But I have several shots I need to take care of and get them printed. Your boss called this morning. He said the place has been closed up for the next ten days. Something about a fire inspector. Are you really working at a place that needs to be shut down by the fire marshal?" Lily told her sister what had happened last night. "Okay, having the fire extinguisher go off over the stove is messy. It'll be more than ten days, I'm betting. They'll have to inspect it before he'll be able to reopen. If they find any of that retardant on anything in the kitchen area, he'll shut you down again."

Lily didn't care how messy it was to clean up. All she could focus on was not having money coming in for ten days or more. Rogue shook her shoulders. She must have said something to her several times. There was a look of complete concern on her face just then.

"Are you going to listen to me now?" Nodding, she said she would. "Good. As I've told you several times, I have enough money to support you and the kids until we get this court thing looked into. If you can hold the fort down while I make a few calls, maybe I can get it resolved before the restaurant reopens, and you won't have to go back. Just chill out. Together we can keep the kids happy and fed. Don't freak out about money, Lily. I told you, I make great money at my job, and I don't have anyone or anything to spend it on but you and the kids. All right? Say it's all right, Lily."

"It's all right." Hugging her sister, something that she was coming to depend on to get her going, she looked at her when they were apart. "I'm also going to call Dad. You're right. I was being selfish to him."

"I never said that." Lily said she knew that too but felt that way. "I have his number. I'll give it to you. Then I'm going to call my buddy. If he can't help us, I'm betting he knows someone that can."

Lily got the number and wondered at the area code. It occurred to her that she had no idea where her dad was living, nor what he was doing with his life. Picking up the phone to call him, she decided that she needed to get help. There wasn't anything she could do alone that wouldn't go much better with help.

Lexi answered the phone on the second ring.

"Hello, Lexi. It's Lily. Is there any way I can talk to my dad for a little bit?" Lexi said he'd just gone to the store, but she'd love to talk to her. "I've a major problem here...."

Telling her everything she had going on, Lily and Lexi were both sobbing by the time her dad was back home and available to talk to her. She wanted her daddy here. After promising Lexi a hug, Lily wanted a hug from her dad too.

~~~

Loman answered the phone with a snarl. Whoever it was, they'd fucking better have good life insurance, because he was going to hunt them down and kill them. When the laughter greeted him on the other end, Loman knew exactly who was calling him.

"Hi-Men. What are you up to?" He smiled and told her he'd forgotten about the nickname. "I nearly did as well, but that's how I have you listed on my phone. Are you still clipping pictures out of magazines and claiming them as your own?"

"Are you still taking pictures of the dead and hoping one of them is the teacher that failed you in art appreciation?" They both laughed. "How are you, Rogue? It's been forever since I spoke to you. At least five years."

"My phone said it was seven. Sheesh, where has all the time gone?" He told her he'd like to know that too. "I did call you for a reason. Not a shitty one like the last time I called you. You were a saint in letting me blow off steam to you. I've never forgotten that."

"It's all right. All of us need a person we can lean on when we're ready to quit the job we were born to do. You've been there for me enough. What's going on? You know I'll do anything I can. I still owe you for my life." She said it was never as much a hardship as he made it out to be, saving his life. "I'm not dead, and you've no idea how many times a day I thank you for that. What do you need?"

"Is Hop-Along still an attorney?" Loman told her he was. He'd forgotten that Cass had been called that in college. He told her he was working for their sister-in-law. "Oh. Then he might not be able to help out my sister and her kids. She's been shafted big time."

After she told him everything going on with Lily and her family, Loman was sure if Cass couldn't help them, he'd find an attorney that could. Rogen really had saved his life long ago. And the beating she'd given him, both physically and verbally, had gotten him on the right track again and made him a better photographer. He would literally lay down his life for her.

"I'm going to see him here in about an hour. Where are you?" She told him she'd rented a house for her sister and kids, but Lily thought they were house-sitting. "She's still as stubborn as I remember her to be, isn't she? Can you get to Ohio? I know my family has a couple of houses here they can let them stay in. No charge."

"I can get there, but shouldn't you talk to your brother first? I mean, he might not be able to help, and I don't want to give up this house. They were living in a one bedroom flat when I found her. The kids literally had nothing but their clothing. This isn't the way to treat any kids if you ask me." Loman wondered what Rogue would do when she found this Missy person. Kill her, more than likely. He knew he would be hard-pressed not to do her some serious damage himself. "You call me when you have his okay that he's going to be able to help her, and we'll be there."

"Cass will help you if for no other reason than I've asked him to. Even if he can't, he'll for sure know someone that can. You guys make your way here. I'm still living in the same town I was in when we were in college. My own home, but in the same town. My dad is dead now, and my mom is finally getting to enjoy life again." Rogue knew the story about his dad and told him congratulations on that. "Yeah, I am thrilled too that

Ronan is now the king of all lions. He's doing a bang-up job at it too. Mom is also getting the party house redone, so perhaps by the time you get here, it'll be open."

"I'd love that. Okay, yeah, I'll get them there. I want to show the kids a good time while we're getting there, so it might take me a few days of driving to make it. It's not that far, I know, but there are a lot of sights we can see on the way. Amish country is going to be one of the places we go too." He had gone there with her once and vowed never again. She bought so much cheese and other things from around the town that there had barely been enough room for him in the car on the way back. "I'm not going to be buying out the cheese market again, Hi-Men. Do you ever think of the things we did while we were supposed to be studying? Christ, what I wouldn't give to go back and actually learn some of the things I had to learn by hard knocks."

"You and me both. But I did go back. I think I read someplace that you did as well." She said she had a good education. "I'm sure, knowing you, it was the best. Okay, I need to get going. A friend of the family lost his mother a few days ago, and we're helping him out by being there for him."

After telling him she was sorry for his loss, they talked for a couple of minutes more. Excited to have her around for a little while, Loman reached out to his brother Cass and told him everything she'd told him. And about her need for a good attorney.

You bet I'll take it. Loman asked him why he said yes so quickly. *I've been keeping up with the backlash of the trial for a while now. It was all over the papers about a year ago how a judge was being looked into about several cases that had been across his desk. Apparently, it was proven that he'd taken quite a few bribes to make some cases fall in favor of the wrong person.*

That's shitty. So you think this will be resolved quickly? Cass told him that nothing was ever a slam dunk in the court system. *I guess I knew that too. She and her family will be here in a few days. She's trying to make sure the kids are shown a good time. I feel really badly for them. To know that their own mother wanted nothing to do with them before or after their dad died.*

Giving Cass the information he'd written down as he spoke to Rogue, he was glad now that he'd always been a good note taker. Some of the more complicated questions his brother asked him he had the answers for. Then he asked how Rogue was doing.

She's still working for the FBI. She has a Ph.D. in Forensic Photography, which is what is making her someone they depend on to help out with a case. I think she's also taking pictures under another name. I've seen her style in a couple of books I've purchased. Rogue has always been a very persistent person, as I remember. I'm betting no one disputes her work, either. She's really good. Cass pointed out that he was as well. *I don't know about that. You should see her working at a crime scene. I've only seen her a couple of times doing it. She's very intense at it.*

Yes, but you are as well. I haven't any idea how you get the shots you do. I swear you must be something akin to a master at it. They both laughed. *I'm going to start on this before they get here. If you want to tell her I'll take the case, that'll be great. Also, I'll have all the transcripts and anything else I can get from the other trial. Her sister really got the shaft on this one.*

Truer words couldn't have been better said. As he was getting dressed for the funeral, he thought about Benson. The man was taking his mom's death better than he would have. Loman thought it was because he had Don there for him, as well as Parker. It also helped that little Pete had taken a great shine to the man. They would sit and stare at one another for hours on end. Loman thought Parker was slightly jealous of the bond the two of them had.

As soon as he made it to the funeral home, he was glad he'd worn his favorite shirt today. There were so many bright colors in the room; it brought a smile to his face. He thought Benson had it right. This wasn't a funeral for his momma, but a party of her life. Even the flowers had taken on a festive theme. He hugged Benson when he saw the young man standing near the casket.

"Mrs. Parker said we were going to have a party later, to help me with bills and stuff. I sure do hope I can do this. Momma wanted me to be able to do things on my own." Loman told him he'd do great. "I hope so. I surely do."

When the service began, he was surprised by all of the football team being there. They'd even volunteered to be pallbearers for their new friend. It was a sight that brought tears to each of the people in the room, to see seventeen teenagers in their new uniforms being there for a man nearly twice their age.

When the service was over, the players each hugged Benson and told him they'd be there for him. Loman had to wipe the tears as they streamed down his cheeks. There wasn't a dry eye in the room when they handed him their phone numbers as they took turns telling Benson how sorry they were for his loss.

On his way home, he thought of his friend Rogue. He wondered if, after all this time, she'd finally found someone to love her. Someone that would treat her well. There were things she'd told him about growing up in a house of gloom that he was sure no one else knew about. The drugs and alcohol that she had indulged in. The things that had kept her going when she'd been just a child.

Looking forward to her coming with a light heart, Loman couldn't wait for the rest of his family to meet her. He and Cass had such memories of their trio of shenanigans. It was a small wonder none of them had ended up in jail.

Then he wondered if she might be a mate to any of the others. That, he thought, would be the greatest thing ever. To have his best friend and ally related to him by marriage. Loman pulled out his college days box and looked through the several hundred pictures he'd taken back then. Christ, it was hard to believe they'd ever been that young.

Before You Go...

HELP AN AUTHOR

write a review

THANK YOU!

Share your voice and help guide other readers to these wonderful books. Even if it's only a line or two, your reviews help readers discover the author's books so they can continue creating stories that you'll love. Log in to your favorite retailer and leave a review. Thank you.

AWARD WINNING, BESTSELLING AUTHOR

Kathi Barton, a winner of the Pinnacle Book Achievement award as well as a best-selling author on Amazon and All Romance books, lives in Nashport, Ohio, with her husband, Paul. When not creating new worlds and romance, Kathi and her husband enjoy camping and going to auctions. She can also be seen at county fairs with her husband, who is an artist and potter.

Her muse, a cross between Jimmy Stewart and Hugh Jackman, brings her stories to life for her readers in a way that has them coming back time and again for more. Her favorite genre is paranormal romance, with a great deal of spice. You can visit Kathi on line and drop her an email if you'd like. She loves hearing from her fans. aaronskiss@gmail.com.

Follow Kathi on her blog: http://kathisbartonauthor.blogspot.com/

www.ingramcontent.com/pod-product-compliance
Lightning Source LLC
Chambersburg PA
CBHW020618180626
46810CB00007B/2840